EXTRA
(ORDINARY)
PEOPLE

EXTRA
(ORDINARY)
PEOPLE

JOANNA RUSS

ST. MARTIN'S PRESS
NEW YORK

EXTRA(ORDINARY) PEOPLE. Copyright © 1984 by Joanna Russ. All rights reserved. Printed in the United States of America. No part of this book may be used or reproduced in any manner whatsoever without written permission except in the case of brief quotations embodied in critical articles or reviews. For information, address St. Martin's Press, 175 Fifth Avenue, New York, N.Y. 10010.

Design by M. Paul

Library of Congress Cataloging in Publication Data

Russ, Joanna, 1937–
    Extra(ordinary) people.

    I. Title.
PS3568.U763E9   1984   813'.54   83-19156
ISBN 0-312-27807-1 (pbk)

This book is dedicated
to my mother, whose love of literature
started it all.

"I began thinking of you as *pnongl.* People"—
[said the alien] "it's dreadful, you think a place is just
wild and then there're people—"

—ALICE SHELDON

Contents

"Today," said the tutor, "we study history."
The schoolkid listened.

EXTRA
(ORDINARY)
PEOPLE

Souls

Deprived of other Banquet
I entertained Myself—

—EMILY DICKINSON

This is the tale of the Abbess Radegunde and what happened
when the Norsemen came. I tell it not as it was told to me
but as I saw it, for I was a child then and the Abbess had
made a pet and errand-boy of me, although the stern old
Wardress, Cunigunt, who had outlived the previous Abbess,
said I was more in the Abbey than out of it and a scandal.
But the Abbess would only say mildly, "Dear Cunigunt, a
scandal at the age of seven?" which was turning it off with a
joke, for she knew how harsh and disliking my new stepmother was to me and my father did not care and I with no
sisters or brothers. You must understand that joking and
calling people "dear" and "my dear" was only her manner;
she was in every way an unusual woman. The previous Abbess, Herrade, had found that Radegunde, who had been
given to her to be fostered, had great gifts and so sent the
child south to be taught, and that has never happened here
before. The story has it that the Abbess Herrade found
Radegunde seeming to read the great illuminated book in

the Abbess's study; the child had somehow pulled it off its stand and was sitting on the floor with the volume in her lap, sucking her thumb and turning the pages with her other hand just as if she were reading.

"Little two-years," said the Abbess Herrade, who was a kind woman, "what are you doing?" She thought it amusing, I suppose, that Radegunde should pretend to read this great book, the largest and finest in the Abbey, which had many, many books, more than any other nunnery or monastery I have ever heard of: a full forty then, as I remember. And then little Radegunde was doing the book no harm.

"Reading, Mother," said the little girl.

"Oh, reading?" said the Abbess, smiling; "Then tell me what are you reading," and she pointed to the page.

"This," said Radegunde, "is a great *D* with flowers and other beautiful things about it, which is to show that *Dominus,* our Lord God, is the greatest thing and the most beautiful and makes everything to grow and be beautiful, and then it goes on to say *Domine nobis pacem,* which means *Give peace to us, O Lord."*

Then the Abbess began to be frightened but she said only, "Who showed you this?" thinking that Radegunde had heard someone read and tell the words or had been pestering the nuns on the sly.

"No one," said the child; "Shall I go on?" and she read page after page of the Latin, in each case telling what the words meant.

There is more to the story, but I will say only that after many prayers the Abbess Herrade sent her foster-daughter far southwards, even to Poitiers, where Saint Radegunde had ruled an Abbey before, and some say even to Rome, and in these places Radegunde was taught all learning, for all the learning there is in the world remains in these places. Radegunde came back a grown woman and nursed the Abbess through her last illness and then became Abbess in her turn. They say that the great folk of the Church down there in the south wanted to keep her because she was such a prodigy of female piety and learning, there where life is safe and comfortable and less rude than it is here, but she said that the gray skies and flooding winters of her birthplace called to her very soul. She often told me the story when I was a child: how headstrong she had been and how defiant, and how she had sickened so desperately for her native land that they had sent her back, deciding that a rude life in the mud of a northern village would be a good cure for such a rebellious soul as hers.

"And so it was," she would say, patting my cheek or tweaking my ear; "See how humble I am now?" for you understand, all this about her rebellious girlhood, twenty years back, was a kind of joke between us. "Don't you do it," she would tell me and we would laugh together, I so heartily at the very idea of my being a pious monk full of learning that I would hold my sides and be unable to speak.

She was kind to everyone. She knew all the languages, not only ours, but the Irish too and the tongues folks speak to the north and south, and Latin and Greek also, and all the other languages in the world, both to read and write. She knew how to cure sickness, both the old women's way with herbs or leeches and out of books also. And never was there a more pious woman! Some speak ill of her now she's gone and say she was too merry to be a good Abbess, but she would say, "Merriment is God's flowers," and when the winter wind blew her headdress awry and showed the gray hair—which happened once; I was there and saw the shocked faces of the Sisters with her—she merely tapped the band back into place, smiling and saying, "Impudent wind! Thou showest thou hast power which is more than our silly human power, for it is from God"—and this quite satisfied the girls with her.

No one ever saw her angry. She was impatient sometimes, but in a kindly way, as if her mind were elsewhere. It was in Heaven, I used to think, for I have seen her pray for hours or sink to her knees—right in the marsh!—to see the wild duck fly south, her hands clasped and a kind of wild joy on her face, only to rise a moment later, looking at the mud on her habit and crying half-ruefully, half in laughter, "Oh, what will Sister Laundress say to me? I am hopeless! Dear child, tell no one; I will say I fell," and then she would clap her hand to her mouth, turning red and laughing even harder, saying, "I *am* hopeless, telling lies!"

The town thought her a saint, of course. We were all happy then, or so it seems to me now, and all lucky and well, with this happiness of having her amongst us burning and blooming in our midst like a great fire around which we could all warm ourselves, even those who didn't know why life seemed so good. There was less illness; the food was better; the very weather stayed mild; and people did not quarrel as they had before her time and do again now. Nor do I think, considering what happened at the end, that all this was nothing but the fancy of a boy who's found his mother, for that's what she was to me; I brought her all the gossip and ran errands when I could and she called me Boy News in Latin; I was happier than I have ever been.

And then one day those terrible beaked prows appeared in our river.

I was with her when the warning came, in the main room of the Abbey tower just after the first fire of the year had been lit in the great hearth; we thought ourselves safe, for they had never been seen so far south and it was too late in the year for any sensible shipman to be in our waters. The Abbey was host to three Irish priests, who turned pale when young Sister Sibihd burst in with the news, crying and wringing her hands; one of the brothers exclaimed a thing in Latin which means "God protect us!" for they had been telling us stories of the terrible sack of the monastery of

Saint Columbanus and how everyone had run away with the precious manuscripts or had hidden in the woods, and that was how Father Cairbre and the two others had decided to go "walk the world," for this (the Abbess had been telling it all to me for I had no Latin) is what the Irish say when they leave their native land to travel elsewhere.

"God protects our souls, not our bodies," said the Abbess Radegunde briskly. She had been talking with the priests in their own language or in the Latin, but this she said in ours so even the women workers from the village would understand. Then she said, "Father Cairbre, take your friends and the younger Sisters to the underground passages; Sister Diemud, open the gates to the villagers; half of them will be trying to get behind the Abbey walls and the others will be fleeing to the marsh. You, Boy News, down to the cellars with the girls." But I did not go and she never saw it; she was up and looking out one of the window slits instantly. So was I. I had always thought the Norsemen's big ships came right up on land—on legs, I supposed—and was disappointed to see that after they came up our river they stayed in the water like other ships and the men were coming ashore by wading in the water, just as if they had been like all other folk. Then the Abbess repeated her order— "Quickly! Quickly!"—and before anyone knew what had happened she was gone from the room. I watched from the tower window; in the turmoil nobody bothered about me. Below, the Abbey grounds and gardens were packed with folk, all stepping on the herb plots and the Abbess's paestum roses, and great logs were being dragged to bar the door set in the stone walls round the Abbey, not high walls, to tell truth, and Radegunde was going quickly through the crowd, crying, Do this! Do that! Stay, thou! Go, thou! and like things.

Then she reached the door and motioned Sister Oddha, the doorkeeper, aside—the old Sister actually fell to her knees in entreaty—and all this, you must understand, was wonderfully pleasant to me. I had no more idea of danger than a puppy. There was some tumult by the door—I think the men with the logs were trying to get in her way—and Abbess Radegunde took out from the neck of her habit her silver crucifix, brought all the way from Rome, and shook it impatiently at those who would keep her in. So of course they let her through at once.

I settled into my corner of the window, waiting for the Abbess's crucifix to bring down God's lightning on those tall, fair men who defied Our Savior and the law and were supposed to wear animal horns on their heads, though these did not (and I found out later that's just a story; that is not what the Norse do). I did hope that the Abbess or Our Lord would wait just a little while before destroying them, for I wanted to get a good look at them before they all died, you understand. I was somewhat disappointed, as they seemed to be wearing breeches with leggings under them and tunics on top, like ordinary folk, and cloaks also, though some did carry swords and axes and there were round shields piled on the beach at one place. But the long hair they had was fine, and the bright colors of their clothes, and the monsters growing out of the heads of the ships were splendid and very frightening, even though one could see that they were only painted, like the pictures in the Abbess's books.

I decided that God had provided me with enough edification and could now strike down the impious strangers.

But He did not.

Instead the Abbess walked alone towards these fierce men, over the stony river bank, as calmly as if she were on a picnic with her girls. She was singing a little song, a pretty tune that I repeated many years later, and a well-traveled man said it was a Norse cradle-song. I didn't know that then, but only that the terrible, fair men, who had looked up in surprise at seeing one lone woman come out of the Abbey (which was barred behind her; I could see that), now began a sort of whispering astonishment among themselves. I saw the Abbess's gaze go quickly from one to the other—we often said that she could tell what was hidden in the soul from one look at the face—and then she picked the skirt of her habit up with one hand and daintily went among the rocks to one of the men—one older than the others, as it proved later, though I could not see so well at the time— and said to him, in his own language:

"Welcome, Thorvald Einarsson, and what do you, good farmer, so far from your own place, with the harvest ripe and the great autumn storms coming on over the sea?" (You may wonder how I knew what she said when I had no Norse; the truth is that Father Cairbre, who had not gone to the cellars after all, was looking out the top of the window while I was barely able to peep out the bottom, and he re- peated everything that was said for the folk in the room, who all kept very quiet.)

Now you could see that the pirates were dumbfounded to hear her speak their own language and even more so that she called one by his name; some stepped backwards and made strange signs in the air and others unsheathed axes or swords and came running towards the Abbess. But this Thorvald Einarsson put up his hand for them to stop and laughed heartily.

"Think!" he said; "There's no magic here, only clever- ness—what pair of ears could miss my name with the lot of you bawling out 'Thorvald Einarsson, help me with this oar'; 'Thorvald Einarsson, my leggings are wet to the knees'; 'Thorvald Einarsson, this stream is as cold as a Fimbul- winter!'"

The Abbess Radegunde nodded and smiled. Then she sat down plump on the river bank. She scratched behind one ear, as I had often seen her do when she was deep in thought. Then she said (and I am sure that this talk was carried on in a loud voice so that we in the Abbey could hear it):

"Good friend Thorvald, you are as clever as the tale I heard of you from your sister's son, Ranulf, from whom I learnt the Norse when I was in Rome, and to show you it was he, he always swore by his gray horse, Lamefoot, and he had a difficulty in his speech; he could not say the sounds as we do and so spoke of you always as 'Torvald.' Is not that so?"

I did not realize it then, being only a child, but the Abbess was—by this speech—claiming hospitality from the man, and had also picked by chance or inspiration the cleverest among these thieves and robbers, for his next words were:

"I am not the leader. There are no leaders here."

He was warning her that they were not his men to control, you see. So she scratched behind her ear again and got up. Then she began to wander, as if she did not know what to do, from one to the other of these uneasy folk—for some backed off and made signs at her still, and some took out their knives—singing her little tune again and walking slowly, more bent over and older and infirm-looking than we had ever seen her, one helpless little woman in black before all those fierce men. One wild young pirate snatched the headdress from her as she passed, leaving her short gray hair bare to the wind; the others laughed and he that had done it cried out:

"Grandmother, are you not ashamed?"

"Why, good friend, of what?" said she mildly.

"Thou art married to thy Christ," he said, holding the headdress covering behind his back, "but this bridegroom of thine cannot even defend thee against the shame of having thy head uncovered! Now if thou wert married to me—"

There was much laughter. The Abbess Radegunde waited until it was over. Then she scratched her bare head and made as if to turn away, but suddenly she turned back upon him with the age and infirmity dropping from her as if they had been a cloak, seeming taller and very grand, as if lit from within by some great fire. She looked directly into his face. This thing she did was something we had all seen, of course, but they had not, nor had they heard that great, grand voice with which she sometimes read the Scriptures to us or talked with us of the wrath of God. I think the young man was frightened, for all his daring. And I know now what I did not then: that the Norse admire courage above all things and that—to be blunt—everyone likes a good story, especially if it happens right in front of your eyes.

"Grandson!"—and her voice tolled like the great bell of God; I think folk must have heard her all the way to the marsh!—"Little grandchild, thinkest thou that the Creator of the World who made the stars and the moon and the sun and our bodies, too, and the change of the seasons and the very earth we stand on—yea, even unto the shit in thy belly!—thinkest thou that such a being has a big house in the sky where he keeps his wives and goes in to fuck them as thou wouldst thyself or like the King of Turkey? Do not dishonor the wit of the mother who bore thee! We are the servants of God, not his wives, and if we tell our silly girls they are married to the Christ it is to make them understand that they must not run off and marry Otto Farmer or Ekkehard Blacksmith, but stick to their work, as they promised. If I told them they were married to an Idea they would not understand me, and neither dost thou."

(Here Father Cairbre, above me in the window, muttered in a protesting way about something.)

Then the Abbess snatched the silver cross from around her neck and put it into the boy's hand, saying: "Give this to thy mother with my pity. She must pull out her hair over such a child."

But he let it fall to the ground. He was red in the face and breathing hard.

"Take it up," she said more kindly, "take it up, boy; it will not hurt thee and there's no magic in it. It's only pure silver and good workmanship; it will make thee rich." When she saw that he would not—his hand went to his knife—she *tched* to herself in a motherly way (or I believe she did, for she waved one hand back and forth as she always did when she made that sound) and got down on her knees—with more difficulty than was truth, I think—saying loudly, "I will stoop, then; I will stoop," and got up, holding it out to him, saying, "Take. Two sticks tied with a cord would serve me as well."

The boy cried, his voice breaking, "My mother is dead and thou art a witch!" and in an instant he had one arm around the Abbess's neck and with the other his knife at her throat. The man Thorvald Einarsson roared "Thorfinn!" but the Abbess only said clearly, "Let him be. I have shamed this man but did not mean to. He is right to be angry."

The boy released her and turned his back. I remember wondering if these strangers could weep. Later I heard—and I swear that the Abbess must have somehow known this or felt it, for although she was no witch, she could probe at a man until she found the sore places in him and that very quickly—that this boy's mother had been known for an adulteress and that no man would own him as a son. It is one thing among those people for a man to have what the Abbess called a concubine and they do not hold the children of such in scorn as we do, but it is a different thing when a married woman has more than one man. Such was Thorfinn's case; I suppose that was what had sent him *viking*. But all this came later; what I saw then—with my nose barely above the window-slit—was that the Abbess slipped her crucifix over the hilt of the boy's sword—she really wished him to have it, you see—and then walked to a

place near the walls of the Abbey but far from the Norsemen. I think she meant them to come to her. I saw her pick
up her skirts like a peasant woman, sit down with legs
crossed, and say in a loud voice:

"Come! Who will bargain with me?"

A few strolled over, laughing, and sat down with her.

"All!" she said, gesturing them closer.

"And why should we all come?" said one who was farthest away.

"Because you will miss a bargain," said the Abbess.

"Why should we bargain when we can take?" said another.

"Because you will only get half," said the Abbess. "The
rest you will not find."

"We will ransack the Abbey," said a third.

"Half the treasure is not in the Abbey," said she.

"And where is it then?" said yet another.

She tapped her forehead. They were drifting over by
twos and threes. I have heard since that the Norse love rid-
dles and this was a sort of riddle; she was giving them good
fun.

"If it is in your head," said the man Thorvald, who was
standing behind the others, arms crossed, "we can get it out,
can we not?" And he tapped the hilt of his knife.

"If you frighten me, I shall become confused and remember nothing," said the Abbess calmly. "Besides, do you
wish to play that old game? You saw how well it worked the
last time. I am surprised at you, Ranulf's mother's-brother."

"I will bargain then," said the man Thorvald, smiling.

"And the rest of you?" said Radegunde. "It must be all
or none; decide for yourselves whether you wish to save
yourselves trouble and danger and be rich," and she deliberately turned her back on them. The men moved down to
the river's edge and began to talk among themselves, dropping their voices so that we could not hear them any more.

Father Cairbre, who was old and short-sighted, cried, "I cannot hear them. What are they doing?" and I cleverly said, "I have good eyes, Father Cairbre," and he held me up to see, so it was just at the time that the Abbess Radegunde was facing the Abbey tower that I appeared in the window. She clapped one hand across her mouth. Then she walked to the gate and called (in a voice I had learned not to disregard; it had often got me a smacked bottom), "Boy News, down! Come down to me here *at once!* And bring Father Cairbre with you."

I was overjoyed. I had no idea that she might want to protect me if anything went wrong. My only thought was that I was going to see it all from wonderfully close by, so I wormed my way, half-suffocated, through the folk in the tower room, stepping on feet and skirts, and having to say every few seconds, "But I *have* to! The Abbess wants me," and meanwhile she was calling outside like an Empress, "Let that boy through! Make a place for that boy! Let the Irish priest through!" until I crept and pushed and complained my way to the very wall itself—no one was going to open the gate for us, of course—and there was a great fuss and finally someone brought a ladder. I was over at once, but the old priest took a longer time, although it was a low wall, as I've said, the builders having been somewhat of two minds about making the Abbey into a true fortress.

Once outside it was lovely, away from all that crowd, and I ran, gloriously pleased, to the Abbess, who said only, "Stay by me, whatever happens," and immediately turned her attention away from me. It had taken so long to get Father Cairbre outside the walls that the tall foreign men had finished their talking and were coming back—all twenty or thirty of them—towards the Abbey and the Abbess Radegunde, and most especially of all, me. I could see Father Cairbre tremble. They did look grim, close by, with their long, wild hair and the brightness of their strange clothes. I remember that they smelled different from us, but cannot remember how after all these years. Then the Abbess spoke to them in that outlandish language of theirs, so strangely light and lilting to hear from their bearded lips, and then she said something in Latin to Father Cairbre, and he said to us, with a shake in his voice:

"This is the priest, Father Cairbre, who will say our bargains aloud in our own tongue so that my people may hear. I cannot deal behind their backs. And this is my foster-baby, who is very dear to me and who is now having his curiosity rather too much satisfied, I think." (I was trying to stand tall like a man but had one hand secretly holding on to her skirt; so that was what the foreign men had chuckled at!) The talk went on, but I will tell it as if I had understood the Norse, for to repeat everything twice would be tedious.

The Abbess Radegunde said, "Will you bargain?"

There was a general nodding of heads, with a look of: After all, why not?

"And who will speak for you?" said she.

A man stepped forward; I recognized Thorvald Einarsson.

"Ah yes," said the Abbess dryly. "The company that has no leaders. Is this leaderless company agreed? Will it abide by its word? I want no treachery-planners, no Breakwords here!"

There was a great mutter at this. The Thorvald man (he *was* big, close up!) said mildly, "I sail with none such. Let's begin."

We all sat down.

"Now," said Thorvald Einarsson, raising his eyebrows, "according to my knowledge of this thing, you begin. And according to my knowledge you will begin by saying that you are very poor."

"But no," said the Abbess, "we are rich." Father Cairbre groaned. A groan answered him from behind the Abbey

walls. Only the Abbess and Thorvald Einarsson seemed unmoved; it was as if these two were joking in some way that
no one else understood. The Abbess went on, saying, "We
are very rich. Within is much silver, much gold, many
pearls, and much embroidered cloth, much fine-woven
cloth, much carved and painted wood, and many books with
gold upon their pages and jewels set into their covers. All
this is yours. But we have more and better: herbs and medi-
cines, ways to keep food from spoiling, the knowledge of
how to cure the sick; all this is yours. And we have more
and better even than this; we have the knowledge of Christ
and the perfect understanding of the soul, which is yours,
too, any time you wish; you have only to accept it."

Thorvald Einarsson held up his hand. "We will stop
with the first," he said, "and perhaps a little of the second.
That is more practical."

"And foolish," said the Abbess politely, "in the usual
way." And again I had the odd feeling that these two were
sharing a joke no one else even saw. She added, "There is
one thing you may not have, and that is the most precious
of all."

Thorvald Einarsson looked inquiring.

"*My people.* Their safety is dearer to me than myself.
They are not to be touched, not a hair on their heads, not
for any reason. Think: you can fight your way into the Abbey
easily enough, but the folk in there are very frightened of
you and some of the men are armed. Even a good fighter is
cumbered in a crowd. You will slip and fall upon each other
without meaning to or knowing that you do so. Heed my
counsel. Why play butcher when you can have treasure
poured into your laps like kings, without work? And after
that there will be as much again, when I lead you to the
hidden place. An earl's mountain of treasure. Think of it!
And to give all this up for slaves, half of whom will get sick
and die before you get them home—and will need to be fed

if they are to be any good. Shame on you for bad advice-
takers! Imagine what you will say to your wives and families:
Here are a few miserable bolts of cloth with blood spots that
won't come out, here are some pearls and jewels smashed
to powder in the fighting, here is a torn piece of embroidery
which was whole until someone stepped on it in the battle,
and I had slaves but they died of illness and I fucked a pretty
young nun and meant to bring her back, but she leapt into
the sea. And oh yes, there was twice as much again and all of
it whole but we decided not to take that. Too much trouble,
you see."

This was a lively story and the Norsemen enjoyed it.
Radegunde held up her hand.

"People!" she called in German, adding, "Sea-rovers,
hear what I say; I will repeat it for you in your tongue," (and
so she did): *"People, if the Norsemen fight us, do not defend
yourselves but smash everything! Wives, take your cooking
knives and shred the valuable cloth to pieces! Men, with
your axes and hammers hew the altars and the carved
wood to fragments! All, grind the pearls and smash the
jewels against the stone floors! Break the bottles of wine!
Pound the gold and silver to shapelessness! Tear to pieces
the illuminated books! Tear down the hangings and burn
them!*

"But" (she added, her voice suddenly mild) "if these
wise men will accept our gifts, let us heap untouched and
spotless at their feet all that we have and hold nothing back,
so that their kinsfolk will marvel and wonder at the shining
and glistering of the wealth they bring back, though it leave
us nothing but our bare stone walls."

If anyone had ever doubted that the Abbess Radegunde
was inspired by God, their doubts must have vanished away,
for who could resist the fiery vigor of her first speech or the
beneficent unction of her second? The Norsemen sat there

with their mouths open. I saw tears on Father Cairbre's cheeks. Then Thorvald Einarsson said, "Abbess—"

He stopped. He tried again but again stopped. Then he shook himself, as a man who has been under a spell, and said:

"Abbess, my men have been without women for a long time."

Radegunde looked surprised. She looked as if she could not believe what she had heard. She looked the pirate up and down, as if puzzled, and then walked around him as if taking his measure. She did this several times, looking at every part of his big body as if she were summing him up while he got redder and redder. Then she backed off and surveyed him again, and with her arms akimbo like a peasant, announced very loudly in both Norse and German:

"What! Have they lost the use of their hands?"

It was irresistible, in its way. The Norse laughed. Our people laughed. Even Thorvald laughed. I did too, though I was not sure what everyone was laughing about. The laughter would die down and then begin again behind the Abbey walls, helplessly, and again die down and again begin. The Abbess waited until the Norsemen had stopped laughing and then called for silence in German until there were only a few snickers here and there. She then said:

"These good men—Father Cairbre, tell the people— these good men will forgive my silly joke. I meant no scandal, truly, and no harm, but laughter is good; it settles the body's waters, as the physicians say. And my people know that I am not always as solemn and good as I ought to be. Indeed I am a very great sinner and scandal-maker. Thorvald Einarsson, do we do business?"

The big man—who had not been so pleased as the others, I can tell you!—looked at his men and seemed to see what he needed to know. He said: "I go in with five men to see what you have. Then we let the poor folk on the grounds go, but not those inside the Abbey. Then we search again. The gate will be locked and guarded by the rest of us; if there's any treachery, the bargain's off."

"Then I will go with you," said Radegunde. "That is very just and my presence will calm the people. To see us together will assure them that no harm is meant. You are a good man, Torvald—forgive me; I call you as your nephew did so often. Come, Boy News, hold on to me.

"Open the gate!" she called then; "All is safe!" and with the five men (one of whom was that young Thorfinn who had hated her so) we waited while the great logs were pulled back. There was little space within, but the people shrank back at the sight of those fierce warriors and opened a place for us.

I looked back and the Norsemen had come in and were standing just inside the walls, on either side the gate, with their swords out and their shields up. The crowd parted for us more slowly as we reached the main tower, with the Abbess repeating constantly, "Be calm, people, be calm. All is well," and deftly speaking by name to this one or that. It was much harder when the people gasped upon hearing the big logs pushed shut with a noise like thunder, and it was very close on the stairs; I heard her say something like an apology in the queer foreign tongue, something that probably meant, "I'm sorry that we must wait." It seemed an age until the stairs were even partly clear and I saw what the Abbess had meant by the cumbering of a crowd; a man might swing a weapon in the press of people but not very far and it was more likely he would simply fall over someone and crack his head. We gained the great room with the big crucifix of painted wood and the little one of pearls and gold, and the scarlet hangings worked in gold thread that I had played robbers behind so often before I learned what real robbers were: these tall, frightening men whose eyes glistened with greed at what I had fancied every village had. Most of the

Sisters had stayed in the great room, but somehow it was
not so crowded, as the folk had huddled back against the
walls when the Norsemen came in. The youngest girls were
all in a corner, terrified—one could smell it, as one can in
people—and when that young Thorfinn went for the little
gold-and-pearl cross, Sister Sibihd cried in a high, cracked
voice, "It is the body of our Christ!" and leapt up, snatching
it from the wall before he could get to it.

"Sibihd!" exclaimed the Abbess, in as sharp a voice as I
had ever heard her use; "Put that back or you will feel the
weight of my hand, I tell you!"

Now it is odd, is it not, that a young woman desperate
enough not to care about death at the hands of a Norse
pirate should nonetheless be frightened away at the threat
of getting a few slaps from her Abbess? But folk are like that.
Sister Sibihd returned the cross to its place (from whence
young Thorfinn took it) and fell back among the nuns, sobbing, "He desecrates Our Lord God!"

"Foolish girl!" snapped the Abbess. "God only can con-
secrate or desecrate; man cannot. That is a piece of metal."

Thorvald said something sharp to Thorfinn, who slowly
put the cross back on its hook with a sulky look which said,
plainer than words: Nobody gives me what I want. Nothing
else went wrong in the big room or the Abbess's study or
the storerooms, or out in the kitchens. The Norsemen were
silent and kept their hands on their swords but the Abbess
kept talking in a calm way in both tongues; to our folk she
said, "See? It is all right but everyone must keep still. God
will protect us." Her face was steady and clear and I believed her a saint, for she had saved Sister Sibihd and the
rest of us.

But this peacefulness did not last, of course. Something
had to go wrong in all that press of people; to this day I do
not know what. We were in a corner of the long refectory,
which is the place where the Sisters or Brothers eat in an

Abbey, when something pushed me into the wall and I fell,
almost suffocated by the Abbess's lying on top of me. My
head was ringing and on all sides there was a terrible roaring sound with curses and screams, a dreadful tumult as if
the walls had come apart and were falling on everyone. I
could hear the Abbess whispering something in Latin over
and over in my ear. There were dull, ripe sounds, worse
than the rest, which I know now to have been the noise
steel makes when it is thrust into bodies. This all seemed to
go on forever and then it seemed to me that the floor was
wet. Then all became quiet. I felt the Abbess Radegunde get
off me. She said:

"So this is how you wash your floors up north." When I
lifted my head from the wet rushes and saw what she meant,
I was very sick into the corner. Then she picked me up in
her arms and held my face against her bosom so that I
would not see but it was no use; I had already seen: all the
people lying about sprawled on the floor with their bellies
coming out, like heaps of dead fish, old Walafrid with an
axe-handle standing out of his chest—he was sitting up with
his eyes shut in a press of bodies that gave him no room to
lie down—and the young beekeeper, Uta, from the village,
who had been so merry, lying on her back with her long
braids and her gown all dabbled in red dye and a great stain
of it on her belly. She was breathing fast and her eyes were
wide open. As we passed her, the noise of her breathing
ceased.

The Abbess said mildly, "Thy people are thorough
housekeepers, Earl Split-gut."

Thorvald Einarsson roared something at us and the Abbess replied softly, "Forgive me, good friend. You protected
me and the boy and I am grateful. But nothing betrays a
man's knowledge of the German like a word that bites, is it
not so? And I had to be sure."

It came to me then that she had called him "Torvald"

and reminded him of his sister's son so that he would feel he must protect us if anything went wrong. But now she would make him angry, I thought, and I shut my eyes tight. Instead he laughed and said in odd, light German, "I did no housekeeping but to stand over you and your pet. Are you not grateful?"

"Oh very, thank you," said the Abbess with such warmth as she might show to a Sister who had brought her a rose from the garden, or another who copied her work well, or when I told her news, or if Ita the cook made a good soup. But he did not know that the warmth was for everyone and so seemed satisfied. By now we were in the garden and the air was less foul; she put me down, although my limbs were shaking, and I clung to her gown, crumpled, stiff, and blood-reeking though it was. She said, "Oh, my God, what a deal of washing hast Thou given us!" She started to walk towards the gate and Thorvald Einarsson took a step towards her. She said, without turning round: "Do not insist, Thorvald, there is no reason to lock me up. I am forty years old and not likely to be running away into the swamp what with my rheumatism and the pain in my knees and the folk needing me as they do."

There was a moment's silence. I could see something odd come into the big man's face. He said quietly:

"I did not speak, Abbess."

She turned, surprised. "But you did. I heard you."

He said strangely, "I did not."

Children can guess sometimes what is wrong and what to do about it without knowing how; I remember saying, very quickly, "Oh, she does that sometimes. My stepmother says old age has addled her wits," and then, "Abbess, may I go to my stepmother and my father?"

"Yes, of course," she said, "run along, Boy News—" and then stopped, looking into the air as if seeing in it something we could not. Then she said very gently, "No, my dear, you had better stay here with me," and I knew, as surely as if I had seen it with my own eyes, that I was not to go to my stepmother or my father because both were dead.

She did things like that, too, sometimes.

For a while it seemed that everyone was dead. I did not feel grieved or frightened in the least, but I think I must have been, for I had only one idea in my head: that if I let the Abbess out of my sight, I would die. So I followed her everywhere. She was let to move about and comfort people, especially the mad Sibihd, who would do nothing but rock and wail, but towards nightfall, when the Abbey had been stripped of its treasures, Thorvald Einarsson put her and me in her study, now bare of its grand furniture, on a straw pallet on the floor, and bolted the door on the outside. She said:

"Boy News, would you like to go to Constantinople, where the Emperor is and the domes of gold and all the splendid pagans? For that is where this man will take me to sell me."

"Oh yes!" said I, and then, "But will he take me, too?"

"Of course," said the Abbess, and so it was settled. Then in came Thorvald Einarsson, saying:

"Thorfinn is asking for you." I found out later that they were waiting for him to die; none other of the Norse had been wounded but a farmer had crushed Thorfinn's chest with an axe and he was expected to die before morning. The Abbess said:

"Is that a good reason to go?" She added, "I mean that he hates me; will not his anger at my presence make him worse?"

Thorvald said slowly, "The folk here say you can sit by the sick and heal them. Can you do that?"

"To my knowledge, not at all," said the Abbess Radegunde, "but if they believe so, perhaps that calms them and makes them better. Christians are quite as foolish as other people, you know. I will come if you want," and though I saw that she was pale with tiredness, she got to her feet. I should say that she was in a plain brown gown taken from one of the peasant women because her own was being washed clean, but to me she had the same majesty as always. And for him too, I think.

Thorvald said, "Will you pray for him or damn him?"

She said, "I do not pray, Thorvald, and I never damn anybody; I merely sit." She added, "Oh let him; he'll scream your ears off if you don't," and this meant me for I was ready to yell for my life if they tried to keep me from her.

They had put Thorfinn in the chapel, a little stone room with nothing left in it now but a plain wooden cross, not worth carrying off. He was lying, his eyes closed, on the stone altar with furs under him, and his face was gray. Every time he breathed there was a bubbling sound, a little, thin, reedy sound, and as I crept closer I saw why, for in the young man's chest was a great red hole with pink things sticking out of it, all crushed, and in the hole one could see something jump and fall, jump and fall, over and over again. It was his heart beating. Blood kept coming from his lips in a froth. I do not know, of course, what either said, for they spoke in the Norse, but I saw what they did and heard much of it talked of between the Abbess and Thorvald Einarsson later, so I will tell it as if I knew.

The first thing the Abbess did was to stop suddenly on the threshold and raise both hands to her mouth as if in horror. Then she cried furiously to the two guards:

"Do you wish to kill your comrade with the cold and damp? Is this how you treat one another? Get fire in here and some woollen cloth to put over him! No, not more skins, you idiots, *wool* to mold to his body and take up the wet. Run now!"

One said sullenly, "We don't take orders from you, Grandma."

"Oh no?" said she. "Then I shall strip this wool dress from my old body and put it over that boy and then sit here all night in my flabby naked skin! What will this child's soul say to God when it departs this flesh? That his friends would not give up a little of their booty so that he might fight for life? Is this your fellowship? Do it, or I will strip myself and shame you both for the rest of your lives!"

"Well, take it from his share," said the one in a low voice, and the other ran out. Soon there was a fire on the hearth and russet-colored woollen cloth—"From my own share," said one of them loudly, though it was a color the least costly, not like blue or red—and the Abbess laid it loosely over the boy, carefully putting it close to his sides but not moving him. He did not look to be in any pain, but his color got no better. But then he opened his eyes and said in such a little voice as a ghost might have, a whisper as thin and reedy and bubbling as his breath:

"You . . . old witch. But I beat you . . . in the end."

"Did you, my dear?" said the Abbess. "How?"

"Treasure," he said, "for my kinfolk. And I lived as a man at last. Fought . . . and had a woman . . . the one here with the big breasts, Sibihd. . . . Whether she liked it or not. That was good."

"Yes, Sibihd," said the Abbess mildly. "Sibihd has gone mad. She hears no one and speaks to no one. She only sits and rocks and moans and soils herself and will not feed herself, although if one puts food in her mouth with a spoon, she will swallow."

The boy tried to frown. "Stupid," he said at last. "Stupid nuns. The beasts do it."

"Do they?" said the Abbess, as if this were a new idea to her. "Now that is very odd. For never yet heard I of a gander

that blacked the goose's eye or hit her over the head with a
stone or stuck a knife in her entrails when he was through.
When God puts it into their hearts to desire one another,
she squats and he comes running. And a bitch in heat will
jump through the window if you lock the door. Poor fools!
Why didn't you camp three hours' down-river and wait? In a
week half the young married women in the village would
have been slipping away at night to see what the foreigners
were like. Yes, and some unmarried ones, and some of my
own girls, too. But you couldn't wait, could you?"

"No," said the boy, with the ghost of a brag. "Better . . .
this way."

"This way," said she. "Oh yes, my dear, old granny
knows about *this* way! Pleasure for the count of three or
four and the rest of it as much joy as rolling a stone uphill."

He smiled a ghostly smile. "You're a whore, grandma."

She began to stroke his forehead. "No, grandbaby," she
said, "but all Latin is not the Church Fathers, you know,
great as they are. One can find a great deal in those strange
books written by the ones who died centuries before Our
Lord was born. Listen," and she leaned closer to him and
said quietly:

> "Syrian dancing girl, how subtly you sway
>   those sensuous limbs,
> Half-drunk in the smoky tavern, lascivious
>   and wanton,
> Your long hair bound back in the Greek way,
>   clashing the castanets in your hands—"

The boy was too weak to do anything but look astonished. Then she said this:

> "I love you so that anyone permitted to sit near
> you and talk to you seems to me like a god; when

I am near you my spirit is broken, my heart shakes, my voice dies, and I can't even speak. Under my skin I flame up all over and I can't see; there's thunder in my ears and I break out in a sweat, as if from fever; I turn paler than cut grass and feel that I am utterly changed; I feel that Death has come near me."

He said, as if frightened. "Nobody feels like that."

"They do," she said.

He said, in feeble alarm, "You're trying to kill me!"

She said, "No, my dear. I simply don't want you to die a virgin."

It was odd, his saying those things and yet holding on to her hand where he had got at it through the woollen cloth; she stroked his head and he whispered, "Save me, old witch."

"I'll do my best," she said. "You shall do your best by not talking and I by not tormenting you any more, and we'll both try to sleep."

"Pray," said the boy.

"Very well," said she, "but I'll need a chair," and the guards—seeing, I suppose, that he was holding her hand—brought in one of the great wooden chairs from the Abbey, which were too plain and heavy to carry off, I think. Then the Abbess Radegunde sat in the chair and closed her eyes. Thorfinn seemed to fall asleep. I crept nearer her on the floor and must have fallen asleep myself almost at once, for the next thing I knew a gray light filled the chapel, the fire had gone out, and someone was shaking Radegunde, who still slept in her chair, her head leaning to one side. It was Thorvald Einarsson and he was shouting with excitement in his strange German, "Woman, how did you do it! How did you do it!"

"Do what?" said the Abbess thickly. "Is he dead?"

"Dead?" exclaimed the Norseman. "He is healed! Healed! The lung is whole and all is closed up about the heart and the shattered pieces of the ribs are grown together! Even the muscles of the chest are beginning to heal!"

"That's good," said the Abbess, still half asleep. "Let me be."

Thorvald shook her again. She said again, "Oh, let me sleep." This time he hauled her to her feet and she shrieked, "My back, my back! Oh, the saints, my rheumatism!" and at the same time a sick voice from under the blue woollens—a sick voice but a man's voice, not a ghost's—said something in Norse.

"Yes, I hear you," said the Abbess; "you must become a follower of the White Christ right away, this very minute. But *Dominus noster,* please do You put it into these brawny heads that I must have a tub of hot water with pennyroyal in it? I am too old to sleep all night in a chair and I am one ache from head to foot."

Thorfinn got louder.

"Tell him," said the Abbess Radegunde to Thorvald in German, "that I will not baptize him and I will not shrive him until he is a different man. All that child wants is someone more powerful than your Odin god or your Thor god to pull him out of the next scrape he gets into. Ask him: Will he adopt Sibihd as his sister? Will he clean her when she soils herself and feed her and sit with his arm about her, talking to her gently and lovingly until she is well again? The Christ does not wipe out our sins only to have us commit them all over again and that is what he wants and what you all want, a God that gives and gives and gives, but God does not give; He takes and takes and takes. He takes away everything that is not God until there is nothing left but God, and none of you will understand that! There is no remission of sins; there is only change and Thorfinn must change before God will have him."

"Abbess, you are eloquent," said Thorvald, smiling, "but why do you not tell him all this yourself?"

"Because I ache so!" said Radegunde, "Oh, do get me into some hot water!" and Thorvald half led and half supported her as she hobbled out. That morning, after she had had her soak—when I cried, they let me stay just outside the door—she undertook to cure Sibihd, first by rocking her in her arms and talking to her, telling her she was safe now, and promising that the Northmen would go soon, and then when Sibihd became quieter, leading her out into the woods with Thorvald as a bodyguard to see that we did not run away, and little dark Sister Hedwic, who had stayed with Sibihd and cared for her. The Abbess would walk for a while in the mild autumn sunshine and then she would direct Sibihd's face upwards by touching her gently under the chin and say, "See? There is God's sky still," and then, "Look, there are God's trees; they have not changed," and telling her that the world was just the same and God still kindly to folk, only a few more souls had joined the Blessed and were happier waiting for us in Heaven than we could ever be, or even imagine being, on the poor earth. Sister Hedwic kept hold of Sibihd's hand. No one paid more attention to me than if I had been a dog, but every time poor Sister Sibihd saw Thorvald she would shrink away and you could see that Hedwic could not bear to look at him at all; every time he came in her sight she turned her face aside, shut her eyes hard, and bit her lower lip. It was a quiet, almost warm day, as autumn can be sometimes, and the Abbess found a few little blue late flowers growing in a sheltered place against a log and put them into Sibihd's hand, speaking of how beautifully and cunningly God had made all things. Sister Sibihd had enough wit to hold on to the flowers, but her eyes stared and she would have stumbled and fallen if Hedwic had not led her.

Sister Hedwic said timidly, "Perhaps she suffers because she has been defiled, Abbess," and then looked ashamed. For a moment the Abbess looked shrewdly at young Sister Hedwic and then at the mad Sibihd. Then she said:

"Dear daughter Sibihd and dear daughter Hedwic, I am now going to tell you something about myself that I have never told to a single living soul but my confessor. Do you know that as a young woman I studied at Avignon and from there was sent to Rome, so that I might gather much learning? Well, in Avignon I read mightily our Christian Fathers but also in the pagan poets, for as it has been said by Ermenrich of Ellwangen: As dung spread upon a field enriches it to good harvest, thus one cannot produce divine eloquence without the filthy writings of the pagan poets. This is true but perilous; only I thought not so, for I was very proud and fancied that if the pagan poems of love left me unmoved that was because I had the gift of chastity right from God Himself and I scorned sensual pleasures and those tempted by them. I had forgotten, you see, that chastity is not given once and for all like a wedding ring that is put on never to be taken off, but is a garden which each day must be weeded, watered, and trimmed anew, or soon there will be only brambles and wilderness.

"As I have said, the words of the poets did not tempt me, for words are only marks on the page with no life save what we give them. But in Rome there were not only the old books, daughters, but something much worse.

"There were statues. Now you must understand that these are not such as you can imagine from our books, like Saint John or the Virgin; the ancients wrought so cunningly in stone that it is like magic; one stands before the marble holding one's breath, waiting for it to move and speak. They are not statues at all but beautiful naked men and women. It is a city of sea-gods pouring water, daughter Sibihd and daughter Hedwic, of athletes about to throw the discus, and runners and wrestlers and young emperors, and the favorites of kings, but they do not walk the streets like real men, for they are all of stone.

"There was one Apollo, all naked, which I knew I should not look on but which I always made some excuse to my companions to pass by, and this statue, although three miles distant from my dwelling, drew me as if by magic. Oh, he was fair to look on! Fairer than any youth alive now in Germany, or in the world, I think. And then all the old loves of the pagan poets came back to me: Dido and Aeneas, the taking of Venus and Mars, the love of the moon, Diana, for the shepherd boy—and I thought that if my statue could only come to life, he would utter honeyed love-words from the old poets and would be wise and brave, too, and what woman could resist him?"

Here she stopped and looked at Sister Sibihd but Sibihd only stared on, holding the little blue flowers. It was Sister Hedwic who cried, one hand pressed to her heart:

"Did you pray, Abbess?"

"I did," said Radegunde solemnly, "and yet my prayers kept becoming something else. I would pray to be delivered from the temptation that was in the statue and then, of course, I would have to think of the statue itself, and then I would tell myself that I must run, like the nymph Daphne, to be armored and sheltered within a laurel tree, but my feet seemed to be already rooted to the ground, and then at the last minute I would flee and be back at my prayers again. But it grew harder each time and at last the day came when I did not flee."

"Abbess, *you?*" cried Hedwic with a gasp. Thorvald, keeping his watch a little way from us, looked surprised. I was very pleased—I loved to see the Abbess astonish people; it was one of her gifts—and at seven I had no knowledge of lust except that my little thing felt good sometimes when I handled it to make water, and what had that to do with statues coming to life or women turning into laurel trees? I was more interested in mad Sibihd, the way children are; I did not know what she might do, or if I should be afraid of her, or, if I should go mad myself, what it would be like. But the Abbess was laughing gently at Hedwic's amazement.

"Why not me?" said the Abbess. "I was young and healthy and had no special grace from God any more than the hens or the cows do! Indeed I burned so with desire for that handsome young hero—for so I had made him in my mind, as a woman might do with a man she has seen a few times on the street—that thoughts of him tormented me waking and sleeping. It seemed to me that because of my vows I could not give myself to this Apollo of my own free will, so I would dream that he took me against my will, and oh, what an exquisite pleasure that was!"

Here Hedwic's blood came all to her face and she covered it with her hands. I could see Thorvald grinning, back where he watched us.

"And then," said the Abbess, as if she had not seen either of them, "a terrible fear came to my heart that God might punish me by sending a ravisher who would use me unlawfully, as I had dreamed my Apollo did, and that I would not even wish to resist him, and would feel the pleasures of a base lust, and would know myself a whore and a false nun forever after. This fear both tormented and drew me. I began to steal looks at young men in the streets, not letting the other Sisters see me do it, thinking: Will it be he? Or he? Or he?

"And then it happened. I had lingered behind the others at a melon-seller's, thinking of no Apollos or handsome heroes but only of the convent's dinner, when I saw my companions disappearing round a corner. I hastened to catch up with them—and made a wrong turning—and was suddenly lost in a narrow street—and at that very moment a young fellow took hold of my habit and threw me to the ground! You may wonder why he should do such a mad thing, but as I found out afterwards, there are prostitutes in Rome who affect our way of dress to please the appetites of certain men who are depraved enough to— Well, really, I do not know how to say it! Seeing me alone, he had thought I was one of them and would be glad of a customer and a bit of play. So there was a reason for it.

"Well, there I was on my back with this young fellow, sent as a vengeance by God, as I thought, trying to do exactly what I had dreamed, night after night, my statue should do. And do you know, it was nothing in the least like my dream! The stones at my back hurt me, for one thing. And instead of melting with delight, I was screaming my head off in terror and kicking at him as he tried to pull up my skirts, and praying to God that this insane man might not break any of my bones in his rage!

"My screams brought a crowd of people and he went running, so I got off with nothing worse than a bruised back and a sprained knee. But the strangest thing of all was that, while I was cured forever of lusting after my Apollo, instead I began to be tormented by a new fear—that I had lusted after *him*, that foolish young man with the foul breath and the one tooth missing!—and I felt strange creepings and crawlings over my body that were half like desire and half like fear and half like disgust and shame with all sorts of other things mixed in—I know that is too many halves, but it is how I felt—and nothing at all like the burning desire I had felt for my Apollo. I went to see the statue once more before I left Rome and it seemed to look at me sadly, as if to say: Don't blame me, poor girl; I'm only a piece of stone. And that was the last time I was so proud as to believe that God had singled me out for a special gift, like chastity—or a special sin, either—or that being thrown down on the ground and hurt had anything to do with any sin of mine, no matter how I mixed the two together in my mind. I dare say you did not find it a great pleasure yesterday, did you?"

Hedwic shook her head. She was crying quietly. She said, "Thank you, Abbess," and the Abbess embraced her. They both seemed happier, but then all of a sudden Sibihd muttered something, so low that one could not hear her.

"The—" she whispered and then she brought it out but still in a whisper: "The blood."

"What, dear, your blood?" said Radegunde.

"No mother," said Sibihd, beginning to tremble, "the blood. All over us. Walafrid and—and Uta—and Sister Hildegarde—and everyone broken and spilled out like a dish! And none of us had done anything but I could smell it all over me and the children screaming because they were being trampled down, and those demons come up from Hell though we had done nothing and—and—I understand, mother, about the rest, but I will never, ever forget it, oh Christ, it is all around me now, oh mother, the *blood!*"

Then Sister Sibihd dropped to her knees on the fallen leaves and began to scream, not covering her face as Sister Hedwic had done, but staring ahead with her wide eyes as if she were blind or could see something we could not. The Abbess knelt down and embraced her, rocking her back and forth, saying, "Yes, yes, dear, but we are here; we are here now; that is gone now," but Sibihd continued to scream, covering her ears as if the scream were someone else's and she could hide herself from it.

Thorvald said, looking, I thought, a little uncomfortable, "Cannot your Christ cure this?"

"No," said the Abbess. "Only by undoing the past. And that is the one thing He never does, it seems. She is in Hell now and must go back there many times before she can forget."

"She would make a bad slave," said the Norseman, with a glance at Sister Sibihd, who had fallen silent and was staring ahead of her again; "You need not fear that anyone will want her."

"God," said the Abbess Radegunde calmly, "is merciful."

Thorvald Einarsson said, "Abbess, I am not a bad man."

"For a good man," said the Abbess Radegunde, "you keep surprisingly bad company."

He said angrily, "I did not choose my shipmates. I have had bad luck!"

"Ours has," said the Abbess, "been worse, I think."

"Luck is luck," said Thorvald, clenching his fists. "It comes to some folk and not to others."

"As you came to us," said the Abbess mildly. "Yes, yes, I see, Thorvald Einarsson; one may say that luck is Thor's doing or Odin's doing, but you must know that our bad luck is your own doing and not some god's. You are our bad luck, Thorvald Einarsson. It's true that you're not as wicked as your friends. for they kill for pleasure and you do it without feeling, as a business, the way one hews down grain. Perhaps you have seen today some of the grain you have cut. If you had a man's soul, you would not have gone *viking,* luck or no luck, and if your soul were bigger still, you would have tried to stop your shipmates, just as I talk honestly to you now, despite your anger, and just as Christ Himself told the truth and was nailed on cross. If you were a beast, you could not break God's law and if you were a man you would not, but you are neither and that makes you a kind of monster that spoils everything it touches and never knows the reason, and that is why I will never forgive you until you become a man, a true man with a true soul. As for your friends—"

Here Thorvald Einarsson struck the Abbess on the face with his open hand and knocked her down. I heard Sister Hedwic gasp in horror, and behind us Sister Sibihd began to moan. But the Abbess only sat there, rubbing her jaw and smiling a little. Then she said:

"Oh, dear, have I been at it again? I am ashamed of myself. You are quite right to be angry, Torvald; no one can stand me when I go on in that way, least of all myself; it is such a bore. Still, I cannot seem to stop it; I am too used to being the Abbess Radegunde, that is clear. I promise never to torment you again, but you, Thorvald, must never strike me again, because you will be very sorry if you do."

He took a step forward.

"No, no, my dear man," the Abbess said merrily, "I mean no threat—how could I threaten you?—I mean only that I will never tell you any jokes, my spirits will droop, and I will become as dull as any other woman. Confess it now: I am the most interesting thing that has happened to you in years and I have entertained you better, sharp tongue and all, than all the *skalds* at the Court of Norway. And I know more tales and stories than they do—more than anyone in the whole world—for I make new ones when the old ones wear out.

"Shall I tell you a story now?"

"About your Christ?" said he, the anger still in his face.

"No," said she, "about living men and women. Tell me, Torvald, what do you men want from us women?"

"To be talked to death," said he, and I could see there was some anger in him still, but he was turning it to play also.

The Abbess laughed in delight. "Very witty!" she said, springing to her feet and brushing the leaves off her skirt. "You are a very clever man, Torvald. I beg your pardon, Thorvald. I keep forgetting. But as to what men want from women, if you asked the young men, they would only wink and dig one another in the ribs, but that is only how they deceive themselves. That is only body calling to body. They themselves want something quite different and they want it

so much that it frightens them. So they pretend it is anything and everything else: pleasure, comfort, a servant in the
home. Do you know what it is that they want?"

"What?" said Thorvald.

"The mother," said Radegunde, "as women do, too; we
all want the mother. When I walked before you on the riverbank yesterday, I was playing the mother. Now you did
nothing, for you are no young fool, but I knew that sooner
or later one of you, so tormented by his longing that he
would hate me for it, would reveal himself. And so he did:
Thorfinn, with his thoughts all mixed up between witches
and grannies and whatnot. I knew I could frighten him, and
through him, most of you. That was the beginning of my
bargaining. You Norse have too much of the father in your
country and not enough mother, with all your honoring of
your women; that is why you die so well and kill other folk
so well—and live so very, very badly."

"You are doing it again," said Thorvald, but I think he
wanted to listen all the same.

"Your pardon, friend," said the Abbess. "You are brave
men; I don't deny it. But I know your *sagas* and they are all
about fighting and dying and afterwards not Heavenly happiness but the end of the world: everything, even the gods,
eaten by the Fenris-wolf and the Midgard snake! What a pity,
to die bravely only because life is not worth living! The Irish
knew better. The pagan Irish were heroes, with their
Queens leading them to battle as often as not, and Father
Cairbre, God rest his soul, was complaining only two days
ago that the common Irish folk were blasphemously making
a goddess out of God's mother, for do they build shrines to
Christ or Our Lord or pray to them? No! It is Our Lady of
the Rocks and Our Lady of the Sea and Our Lady of the
Grove and Our Lady of this or that from one end of the land
to the other. And even here it is only the Abbey folk who
speak of God the Father and of Christ. In the village if one is

sick or another in trouble it is: Holy Mother, save me! and: *Mariam Virginem,* intercede for me, and: Blessed Virgin, blind my husband's eyes! and: Our Lady, preserve my crops, and so on, men and women both. We all need the mother."

"You, too?"

"More than most," said the Abbess.

"And I?"

"Oh no," said the Abbess, stopping suddenly, for we had all been walking slowly back towards the village as she spoke. "No, and that is what drew me to you at once. I saw it in you and knew you were the leader. It is followers who make leaders, you know, and your shipmates have made you leader, whether you know it or not. What you want is—how shall I say it? You are a clever man, Thorvald, perhaps the cleverest man I have ever met, more even than the scholars I knew in my youth. But your cleverness has had no food. It is a cleverness of the world and not of books. You want to travel and know about folk and their customs, and what strange places are like, and what has happened to men and women in the past. If you take me to Constantinople, it will not be to get a price for me but merely to go there; you went seafaring because this longing itched at you until you could bear it not a year more; I know that."

"Then you are a witch," said he, and he was not smiling.

"No, I only saw what was in your face when you spoke of that city," said she. "Also there is gossip that you spent much time in Göteborg as a young man, idling and dreaming and marveling at the ships and markets when you should have been at your farm."

She said, "Thorvald, I can feed that cleverness. I am the wisest woman in the world. I know everything—everything! I know more than my teachers; I make it up or it comes to me, I don't know how, but it is real—real!—and I know more than anyone. Take me from here, as your slave if you wish but as your friend also, and let us go to Constantinople and see the domes of gold, and the walls all inlaid with gold, and the people so wealthy you cannot imagine it, and the whole city so gilded it seems to be on fire, and pictures as high as a wall, set right in the wall and all made of jewels so there is nothing else like them, redder than the reddest rose, greener than the grass, and with a blue that makes the sky pale!"

"You are indeed a witch," said he, "and not the Abbess Radegunde."

She said slowly, "I think I am forgetting how to be the Abbess Radegunde."

"Then you will not care about them any more," said he and pointed to Sister Hedwic, who was still leading the stumbling Sister Sibihd.

The Abbess's face was still and mild. She said, "I care. Do not strike me, Thorvald, not ever again, and I will be a good friend to you. Try to control the worst of your men and leave as many of my people free as you can—I know them and will tell you which can be taken away with the least hurt to themselves or others—and I will feed that curiosity and cleverness of yours until you will not recognize this old world any more for the sheer wonder and awe of it; I swear this on my life."

"Done," said he, adding, "but with my luck, your life is somewhere else, locked in a box on top of a mountain, like the troll's in the story, or you will die of old age while we are still at sea."

"Nonsense," she said, "I am a healthy mortal woman with all my teeth, and I mean to gather many wrinkles yet."

He put his hand out and she took it; then he said, shaking his head in wonder, "If I sold you in Constantinople, within a year you would become Queen of the place!"

The Abbess laughed merrily and I cried in fear, "Me, too! Take me too!" and she said, "Oh yes, we must not forget little Boy News," and lifted me into her arms. The frightening tall man, with his face close to mine, said in his strange sing-song German:

"Boy, would you like to see the whales leaping in the open sea and the seals barking on the rocks? And cliffs so high that a giant could stretch his arms up and not reach their tops? And the sun shining at midnight?"

"Yes!" said I.

"But you will be a slave," he said, "and may be ill-treated and will always have to do as you are bid. Would you like that?"

"No!" I cried lustily, from the safety of the Abbess's arms; "I'll fight!"

He laughed a mighty, roaring laugh and tousled my head—rather too hard, I thought—and said, "I will not be a bad master, for I am named for Thor Red-beard and he is strong and quick to fight but good-natured, too, and so am I," and the Abbess put me down and so we walked back to the village, Thorvald and the Abbess Radegunde talking of the glories of this world and Sister Hedwic saying softly, "She is a saint, our Abbess, a saint, to sacrifice herself for the good of the people," and all the time behind us, like a memory, came the low, witless sobbing of Sister Sibihd, who was in Hell.

When we got back we found that Thorfinn was better and the Norsemen were to leave in the morning. Thorvald had a second pallet brought into the Abbess's study and slept on the floor with us that night. You might think his men would laugh at this, for the Abbess was an old woman, but I think he had been with one of the young ones before he came to us. He had that look about him. There was no bedding for the Abbess but an old brown cloak with holes in it, and she and I were wrapped in it when he came in and threw himself down, whistling, on the other pallet. Then he said:

"Tomorrow, before we sail, you will show me the old Abbess's treasure."

"No," said she. "That agreement was broken."

He had been playing with his knife and now ran his thumb along the edge of it. "I can make you do it."

"No," said she patiently, "and now I am going to sleep."

"So you make light of death?" he said. "Good! That is what a brave woman should do, as the *skalds* sing, and not move, even when the keen sword cuts off her eyelashes. But what if I put this knife here not to your throat but to your little boy's? You would tell me then quick enough!"

The Abbess turned away from him, yawning and saying, "No, Thorvald, because you would not. And if you did, I would despise you for a cowardly oathbreaker and not tell you for that reason. Good night."

He laughed and whistled again for a bit. Then he said: "Was all that true?"

"All what?" said the Abbess. "Oh, about the statue. Yes, but there was no ravisher. I put him in the tale for poor Sister Hedwic."

Thorvald snorted, as if in disappointment. "Tale? You tell lies, Abbess!"

The Abbess drew the old brown cloak over her head and closed her eyes. "It helped her."

Then there was a silence, but the big Norseman did not seem able to lie still. He shifted this way and that, stared at the ceiling, turned over, shifted his body again as if the straw bothered him, and again turned over. He finally burst out, "But what happened!"

She sat up. Then she shut her eyes. She said, "Maybe it does not come into your man's thoughts that an old woman gets tired and that the work of dealing with folk is hard work, or even that it is work at all. Well!

"Nothing 'happened,' Thorvald. Must something happen only if this one fucks that one or one bangs in another's head? I desired my statue to the point of such foolishness that I determined to find a real, human lover, but when I raised my eyes from my fancies to the real, human men of Rome and unstopped my ears to listen to their talk, I realized that the thing was completely and eternally impossible. Oh, those younger sons with their skulking, jealous hatred of the rich, and the rich ones with their noses in the air because they thought themselves of such great consequence because of their silly money, and the timidity of the priests to their superiors, and their superiors' pride, and the artisans' hatred of the peasants, and the peasants being worked like animals from morning until night, and half the men I saw beating their wives and the other half out to cheat some poor girl of her money or her virginity or both—this was enough to put out any fire! And the women doing less harm only because they had less power to do harm, or so it seemed to me then. So I put all away, as one does with any disappointment. Men are not such bad folk when one stops expecting them to be gods, but they are not for me. If that state is chastity, then a weak stomach is temperance, I think. But whatever it is, I have it, and that's the end of the matter."

"*All* men?" said Thorvald Einarsson with his head to one side, and it came to me that he had been drinking, though he seemed sober.

"Thorvald," said the Abbess, "what you want with this middle-aged wreck of a body I cannot imagine, but if you lust after my wrinkles and flabby breasts and lean, withered flanks, do whatever you want quickly and then for Heaven's sake, let me sleep. I am tired to death."

He said in a low voice, "I need to have power over you."

She spread her hands in a helpless gesture. "Oh Thorvald, Thorvald, I am a weak little woman over forty years old! Where is the power? All I can do is talk!"

He said, "That's it. That's how you do it. You talk and talk and talk and everyone does just as you please; I have seen it!"

The Abbess said, looking sharply at him, "Very well. If you must. *But if I were you, Norseman, I would as soon bed my own mother.* Remember that as you pull my skirts up."

That stopped him. He swore under his breath, turning over on his side, away from us. Then he thrust his knife into the edge of his pallet, time after time. Then he put the knife under the rolled-up cloth he was using as a pillow. We had no pillow so I tried to make mine out of the edge of the cloak and failed. Then I thought that the Norseman was afraid of God working in Radegunde, and then I thought of Sister Hedwic's changing color and wondered why. And then I thought of the leaping whales and the seals, which must be like great dogs because of the barking, and then the seals jumped on land and ran to my pallet and lapped at me with great icy tongues of water so that I shivered and jumped and then I woke up.

The Abbess Radegunde had left the pallet—it was her warmth I had missed—and was walking about the room. She would step and pause, her skirts making a small noise as she did so. She was careful not to touch the sleeping Thorvald. There was a dim light in the room from the embers that still glowed under the ashes in the hearth, but no light came from between the shutters of the study window, now shut against the cold. I saw the Abbess kneel under the plain wooden cross which hung on the study wall and heard her say a few words in Latin; I thought she was praying. But then she said in a low voice:

"'Do not call upon Apollo and the Muses, for they are deaf things and vain.' But so are you, Pierced Man, deaf and vain."

Then she got up and began to pace again. Thinking of it

now frightens me, for it was the middle of the night and no one to hear her—except me, but she thought I was asleep—and yet she went on and on in that low, even voice as if it were broad day and she were explaining something to someone, as if things that had been in her thoughts for years must finally come out. But I did not find anything alarming in it then, for I thought that perhaps all Abbesses had to do such things, and besides she did not seem angry or hurried or afraid; she sounded as calm as if she were discussing the profits from the Abbey's bee-keeping—which I had heard her do—or the accounts for the wine cellars—which I had also heard—and there was nothing alarming in that. So I listened as she continued walking about the room in the dark. She said:

"Talk, talk, talk, and always to myself. But one can't abandon the kittens and puppies; that would be cruel. And being the Abbess Radegunde at least gives one something to do. But I am so sick of the good Abbess Radegunde; I have put on Radegunde every morning of my life as easily as I put on my smock, and then I have had to hear the stupid creature praised all day!—sainted Radegunde, just Radegunde who is never angry or greedy or jealous, kindly Radegunde who sacrifices herself for others and always the talk, talk, talk, bubbling and boiling in my head with no one to hear or understand, and no one to answer. No, not even in the south, only a line here or a line there, and all written by the dead. Did they feel as I do? That the world is a giant nursery full of squabbles over toys and the babes thinking me some kind of goddess because I'm not greedy for their dolls or bits of straw or their horses made of tied-together sticks?

"Poor people, if only they knew! It's so easy to be temperate when one enjoys nothing, so easy to be kind when one loves nothing, so easy to be fearless when one's life is no better than one's death. And so easy to scheme when the success or failure of the scheme doesn't matter.

"Would they be surprised, I wonder, to find out what my real thoughts were when Thorfinn's knife was at my throat? Curiosity! But he would not do it, of course; he does everything for show. And they would think I was twice holy, not to care about death.

"Then why not kill yourself, impious Sister Radegunde? Is it your religion which stops you? Oh, you mean the holy wells, and the holy trees, and the blessed saints with their blessed relics, and the stupidity that shamed Sister Hedwic and the promises of safety that drove poor Sibihd mad when the blessed body of her Lord did not protect her and the blessed love of the blessed Mary turned away the sharp point of not one knife? Trash! Idle leaves and sticks, reeds and rushes, filth we sweep off our floors when it grows too thick. As if holiness had anything to do with all of that. As if every place were not as holy as every other and every thing as holy as every other, from the shit in Thorfinn's bowels to the rocks on the ground. As if all places and things were not clouds placed in front of our weak eyes, to keep us from being blinded by that glory, that eternal shining, that blazing all about us, that torrent of light that is everything and is in everything! That is what keeps me from the river, but it never speaks to me or tells me what to do, and to it good and evil are the same—no, it is something else than good or evil; it *is,* only—so it is not God. That I know.

"So, people, is your Radegunde a witch or a demon? Is she full of pride or is Radegunde abject? Perhaps she is a witch. Once, long ago, I confessed to Old Gerbertus that I could see things that were far away merely by closing my eyes, and I proved it to him, too, and he wept over me and gave me much penance, crying, 'If it come of itself it may be a gift of God, daughter, but it is more likely the work of a demon, so do not do it!' And then we prayed and I told him the power had left me, to make the poor old puppy less troubled in its mind, but that was not true, of course. I could still see Turkey as easily as I could see him, and places far beyond: the squat wild men of the plains on their ponies, and the strange tall people beyond that with their great cities and odd eyes, as if one pulled one's eyelid up on a slant, and then the seas with the great wild lands and the cities more full of gold than Constantinople, and then the water again until one comes back home, for the world's a ball, as the ancients said.

"But I did stop somehow, over the years. Radegunde never had time, I suppose. Besides, when I opened that door it was only pictures, as in a book, and all to no purpose, and after a while I had seen them all and no longer cared for them. It is the other door that draws me, when it opens itself but a crack and strange things peep through, like Ranulf sister's-son and the name of his horse. That door is good but very heavy; it always swings back after a little. I shall have to be on my deathbed to open it all the way, I think.

"The fox is asleep. He is the cleverest yet; there is something in him so that at times one can almost talk to him. But still a fox, for the most part. Perhaps in time . . .

"But let me see; yes, he is asleep. And the Sibihd puppy is asleep, though it will be having a bad dream soon, I think, and the Thorfinn kitten is asleep, as full of fright as when it wakes, with its claws going in and out, in and out, lest something strangle it in its sleep."

Then the Abbess fell silent and moved to the shuttered window as if she were looking out, so I thought that she was indeed looking out—but not with her eyes—at all the sleeping folk, and this was something she had done every night of her life to see if they were safe and sound. But would she not know that *I* was awake? Should I not try very hard to get to sleep before she caught me? Then it seemed to me that she smiled in the dark, although I could not see it. She said in that same low, even voice: "Sleep or wake, Boy News; it is all one to me. Thou hast heard nothing of any importance, only the silly Abbess talking to herself, only Radegunde saying goodbye to Radegunde, only Radegunde going away—don't cry, Boy News; I am still here—but there: Radegunde has gone. This Norseman and I are alike in one way: our minds are like great houses with many of the rooms locked shut. We crowd in a miserable huddled few, like poor folk, when we might move freely among them all, as gracious as princes. It is fate that locked away so much of the Norseman from the Norseman—see, Boy News, I do not say his name, not even softly, for that wakes folks—but I wonder if the one who bolted me in was not Radegunde herself, she and Old Gerbertus—whom I partly believed—they and the years and years of having to be Radegunde and do the things Radegunde did and pretend to have the thoughts Radegunde had and the endless, endless lies Radegunde must tell everyone, and Radegunde's utter and unbearable loneliness."

She fell silent again. I wondered at the Abbess's talk this time: saying she was not there when she was, and about living locked up in small rooms—for surely the Abbey was the most splendid house in all the world and the biggest—and how could she be lonely when all the folk loved her? But then she said in a voice so low that I could hardly hear it:

"Poor Radegunde! So weary of the lies she tells and the fooling of men and women with the collars round their necks and bribes of food for good behavior and a careful twitch of the leash that they do not even see or feel. And with the Norseman it will be all the same: lies and flattery and all of it work that never ends and no one ever even sees, so that finally Radegunde will lie down like an ape in a cage, weak and sick from hunger, and will never get up.

"Let her die now. There: Radegunde is dead. Radegunde is gone. Perhaps the door was heavy only because she was on the other side of it, pushing against me. Perhaps it will open all the way now. I have looked in all directions: to the east, to the north and south, and to the west, but there is one place I have never looked and now I will: away from the ball, straight up. Let us see—"

She stopped speaking all of a sudden. I had been falling asleep, but this silence woke me. Then I heard the Abbess gasp terribly, like one mortally stricken, and then she said in a whisper so keen and thrilling that it made the hair stand up on my head: *Where art thou?* The next moment she had torn the shutters open and was crying out with all her voice: *Help me! Find me! Oh come, come, come, or I die!*

This waked Thorvald. With some Norse oath he stumbled up and flung on his sword-belt, and then put his hand to his dagger; I had noticed this thing with the dagger was a thing Norsemen liked to do. The Abbess was silent. He let out his breath in an oof! and went to light the tallow dip at the live embers under the hearth-ashes; when the dip had smoked up, he put it on its shelf on the wall.

He said in German, "What the devil, woman! What has happened?"

She turned round. She looked as if she could not see us, as if she had been dazed by a joy too big to hold, like one who has looked into the sun and is still dazzled by it so that everything seems changed, and the world seems all God's and everything in it like Heaven. She said softly, with her arms around herself, hugging herself: "My people. The real people."

"What are you talking of!" said he.

She seemed to see him then, but only as Sibihd had beheld us; I do not mean in horror as Sibihd had, but beholding through something else, like someone who comes from a vision of bliss which still lingers about her. She said in the same soft voice, "They are coming for me, Thorvald. Is it not wonderful? I knew all this year that something would happen, but I did not know it would be the one thing I wanted in all the world."

He grasped his hair. *"Who* is coming?"

"My people," she said, laughing softly. "Do you not feel them? I do. We must wait three days, for they come from very far away. But then—oh, you will see!"

He said, "You've been dreaming. We sail tomorrow."

"Oh no," said the Abbess simply. "You cannot do that for it would not be right. They told me to wait; they said if I went away, they might not find me."

He said slowly, "You've gone mad. Or it's a trick."

"Oh no, Thorvald," said she. "How could I trick you? I am your friend. And you will wait these three days, will you not, because you are my friend also."

"You're mad," he said, and started for the door of the study, but she stepped in front of him and threw herself on her knees. All her cunning seemed to have deserted her, or perhaps it was Radegunde who had been the cunning one. This one was like a child. She clasped her hands and tears came out of her eyes; she begged him, saying:

"Such a little thing, Thorvald, only three days! And if they do not come, why then we will go anywhere you like, but if they do come you will not regret it, I promise you; they are not like the folk here and that place is like nothing here. It is what the soul craves, Thorvald!"

He said, "Get up, woman, for your God's sake!"

She said, smiling in a sly, frightened way through her blubbered face, "If you let me stay, I will show you the old Abbess's buried treasure, Thorvald."

He stepped back, the anger clear in him. "So this is the brave old witch who cares nothing for death!" he said. Then he made for the door, but she was up again, as quick as a snake, and had flung herself across it.

She said, still with that strange innocence, "Do not strike me. Do not push me. I am your friend!"

He said, "You mean that you lead me by a string round the neck, like a goose. Well, I am tired of that!"

"But I cannot do that any more," said the Abbess breathlessly, "not since the door opened. I am not able now." He raised his arm to strike her and she cowered, wailing, "Do not strike me! Do not push me! Do not, Thorvald!"

He said, "Out of my way then, old witch!"

She began to cry in sobs and gulps. She said, "One is here but another will come! One is buried but another will rise! She will come, Thorvald!" and then in a low, quick voice, "Do not push open this last door. There is one behind it who is evil and I am afraid"—but one could see that he was angry and disappointed and would not listen. He struck her for a second time and again she fell, but with a desperate cry, covering her face with her hands. He unbolted the door and stepped over her and I heard his footsteps go down the corridor. I could see the Abbess clearly—at that time I did not wonder how this could be, with the shadows from the tallow dip half hiding everything in their drunken dance—but I saw every line in her face as if it had been full day and in that light I saw Radegunde go away from us at last.

Have you ever been at some great King's court or some Earl's and heard the story-tellers? There are those so skilled in the art that they not only speak for you what the person in the tale said and did, but they also make an action with their faces and bodies as if they truly were that man or woman, so that it is a great surprise to you when the tale ceases, for you almost believe that you have seen the tale happen in front of your very eyes and it is as if a real man or woman had suddenly ceased to exist, for you forget that all this was only a teller and a tale.

So it was with the woman who had been Radegunde.

She did not change; it was still Radegunde's gray hairs and wrinkled face and old body in the peasant woman's brown dress, and yet at the same time it was a stranger who stepped out of the Abbess Radegunde as out of a gown dropped to the floor. This stranger was without feeling, though Radegunde's tears still stood on her cheeks, and there was no kindness or joy in her. She got up without taking care of her dress where the dirty rushes stuck to it; it was as if the dress were an accident and did not concern her. She said in a voice I had never heard before, one with no feeling in it, as if I did not concern her or Thorvald Einarsson either, as if neither of us were worth a second glance:

"Thorvald, turn around."

Far up in the hall something stirred.

"Now come back. This way."

There were footsteps, coming closer. Then the big Norseman walked clumsily into the room—jerk! jerk! jerk! at every step as if he were being pulled by a rope. Sweat beaded his face. He said, "You—how?"

"By my nature," she said. "Put up the right arm, fox. Now the left. Now both down. Good."

"You—troll!" he said.

"That is so," she said. "Now listen to me, you. There's a man inside you but he's not worth getting at; I tried moments ago when I was new-hatched and he's buried too deep, but now I have grown beak and claws and care nothing for him. It's almost dawn and your boys are stirring; you will go out and tell them that we must stay here another three days. You are weatherwise; make up some story they will believe. And don't try to tell anyone what happened here tonight; you will find that you cannot."

"Folk—come," said he, trying to turn his head, but the effort only made him sweat.

She raised her eyebrows. "Why should they? No one

has heard anything. Nothing has happened. You will go out and be as you always are and I will play Radegunde. For three days only. Then you are free."

He did not move. One could see that to remain still was very hard for him; the sweat poured and he strained until every muscle stood out. She said:

"Fox, don't hurt yourself. And don't push me; I am not fond of you. My hand is light upon you only because you still seem to me a little less unhuman than the rest; do not force me to make it heavier. To be plain: I have just broken Thorfinn's neck, for I find that the change improves him. Do not make me do the same to you."

"No worse . . . than death," Thorvald brought out.

"Ah no?" said she, and in a moment he was screaming and clawing at his eyes. She said, "Open them, open them; your sight is back," and then, "I do not wish to bother myself thinking up worse things, like worms in your guts. Or do you wish dead sons and a dead wife? Now go.

"As you always do," she added sharply, and the big man turned and walked out. One could not have told from looking at him that anything was wrong.

I had not been sorry to see such a bad man punished, one whose friends had killed our folk and would have taken them for slaves—yet I was sorry, too, in a way, because of the seals barking and the whales—and he *was* splendid, after a fashion—and yet truly I forgot all about that the moment he was gone, for I was terrified of this strange person or demon or whatever it was, for I knew that whoever was in the room with me was not the Abbess Radegunde. I knew also that it could tell where I was and what I was doing, even if I made no sound, and was in a terrible riddle as to what I ought to do when soft fingers touched my face. It was the demon, reaching swiftly and silently behind her.

And do you know, all of a sudden everything was all right! I don't mean that she was the Abbess again—I still had very serious suspicions about that—but all at once I felt light as air and nothing seemed to matter very much because my stomach was full of bubbles of happiness, just as if I had been drunk, only nicer. If the Abbess Radegunde were really a demon, what a joke that was on her people! And she did not, now that I came to think of it, seem a bad sort of demon, more the frightening kind than the killing kind, except for Thorfinn, of course, but then Thorfinn had been a very wicked man. And did not the angels of the Lord smite down the wicked? So perhaps the Abbess was an angel of the Lord and not a demon, but if she were truly an angel, why had she not smitten the Norsemen down when they first came and so saved all our folk? And then I thought that, whether angel or demon, she was no longer the Abbess and would love me no longer, and if I had not been so full of the silly happiness which kept tickling about inside me, this thought would have made me weep.

I said, "Will the bad Thorvald get free, demon?"

"No," she said. "Not even if I sleep."

I thought: *But she does not love me.*

"I love thee," said the strange voice, but it was not the Abbess Radegunde's and so was without meaning, but again those soft fingers touched me and there was some kindness in them, even if it was a stranger's kindness.

Sleep, they said.

So I did.

The next three days I had much secret mirth to see the folk bow down to the demon and kiss its hands and weep over it because it had sold itself to ransom them. That is what Sister Hedwic told them. Young Thorfinn had gone out in the night to piss and had fallen over a stone in the dark and broken his neck, which secretly rejoiced our folk, and his comrades did not seem to mind much either, save for one young fellow who had been Thorfinn's friend, I think, and so went about with a long face. Thorvald locked me up in the Abbess's study with the demon every night and went out—or so folk said—to one of the young women, but on those nights the demon was silent and I lay there with the secret tickle of merriment in my stomach, caring about nothing.

On the third morning I woke sober. The demon—or the Abbess—for in the day she was so like the Abbess Radegunde that I wondered—took my hand and walked us up to Thorvald, who was out picking the people to go aboard the Norsemen's boats at the riverbank to be slaves. Folk were standing about weeping and wringing their hands; I thought this strange, because of the Abbess's promise to pick those whose going would hurt least, but I know now that least is not none. The weather was bad, cold rain out of mist, and some of Thorvald's companions were speaking sourly to him in the Norse, but he talked them down—bluff and hearty—as if making light of the weather. The demon stood by him and said, in German, in a low voice so that none might hear: "You will say we go to find the Abbess's treasure and then you will go with us into the woods."

He spoke to his fellows in Norse and they frowned; but the end of it was that two must come with us, for the demon said it was such a treasure as three might carry. The demon had the voice and manner of the Abbess Radegunde, all smiles, so they were fooled. Thus we started out into the trees behind the village, with the rain worse and the ground beginning to soften underfoot. As soon as the village was out of sight the two Norsemen fell behind, but Thorvald did not seem to notice this; I looked back and saw the first man standing in the mud with one foot up, like a goose, and the second with his head lifted and his mouth open so that the rain fell in it. We walked on, the earth sucking at our shoes and all of us getting wet: Thorvald's hair stuck fast against his face and the demon's old brown cloak clinging to its body. Then suddenly the demon began to breathe harshly and it put its hand to its side with a cry. Its cloak fell off and it stumbled before us between the wet trees, not weeping but breathing hard. Then I saw, ahead of us through the pelting rain, a kind of shining among the bare tree-trunks, and as we came nearer the shining became more clear until it was very plain to see, not a blazing thing like a fire at night but a mild and even brightness as though the sunlight were coming through the clouds pleasantly but without strength, as it often does at the beginning of the year.

And then there were folk inside the brightness, both men and women, all dressed in white, and they held out their arms to us and the demon ran to them, crying out loudly and weeping, but paying no mind to the tree-branches which struck it across the face and body. Sometimes it fell but it quickly got up again. When it reached the strange folk they embraced it and I thought that the filth and mud of its gown would stain their white clothing, but the foulness dropped off and would not cling to those clean garments. None of the strange folk spoke a word, nor did the Abbess—I knew then that she was no demon, whatever she was—but I felt them talk to one another, as if in my mind, although I know not how this could be nor the sense of what they said. An odd thing was that as I came closer I could see they were not standing on the ground, as in the way of nature, but higher up, inside the shining, and that their white robes were nothing at all like ours, for they clung to the body so that one might see the people's legs all the way up to the place where the legs joined, even the women's. And some of the folk were like us, but most had a darker color and some looked as if they had been smeared with soot—there are such persons in the far parts of the world, you know, as I found out later; it is their own natural color—and there were some with the odd eyes the Abbess had spoken of—but the oddest thing of all I will not tell you now. When the Abbess had embraced and kissed them all and all had wept, she turned and looked down upon us: Thorvald standing there as if held by a rope and I, who had lost my fear and had crept close in pure awe, for there was such a joy about these people, like the light about them, mild as spring light and yet as strong as in a spring where the winter has gone forever.

"Come to me, Thorvald," said the Abbess, and one could not see from her face if she loved or hated him. He moved closer—jerk! jerk!—and she reached down and touched his forehead with her fingertips, at which one side of his lip lifted, as a dog's does when it snarls.

"As thou knowest," said the Abbess quietly, "I hate thee and would be revenged upon thee. Thus I swore to myself three days ago, and such vows are not lightly broken."

I saw him snarl again and he turned his eyes from her.

"I must go soon," said the Abbess, unmoved, "for I could stay here long years only as Radegunde and Radegunde is no more; none of us can remain here long as our proper selves or even in our true bodies, for if we do we go mad like Sibihd or walk into the river and drown or stop our own hearts, so miserable, wicked, and brutish does your world seem to us. Nor may we come in large companies, for we are few and our strength is not great and we have much to learn and study of thy folk so that we may teach and help without marring all in our ignorance. And ignorant or wise, we can do naught except thy folk aid us.

"Here is my revenge," said the Abbess, and he seemed to writhe under the touch of her fingers, for all they were so light; "Henceforth be not Thorvald Farmer nor yet Thorvald Seafarer but Thorvald Peacemaker, Thorvald War-hater, put into anguish by bloodshed and agonized at cruelty. I cannot make long thy life—that gift is beyond me—but I give thee this: to the end of thy days, long or short, thou wilt know the Presence about thee always, as I do, and thou wilt know that it is neither good nor evil, as I do, and this knowing will trouble and frighten thee always, as it does me, and so about this one thing, as about many another, Thorvald Peacemaker will never have peace.

"Now, Thorvald, go back to the village and tell thy comrades I was assumed into the company of the saints, straight up to Heaven. Thou mayst believe it, if thou wilt. That is all my revenge."

Then she took away her hand and he turned and walked from us like a man in a dream, holding out his hands as if to feel the rain and stumbling now and again, as one who wakes from a vision.

Then I began to grieve, for I knew she would be going away with the strange people and it was to me as if all the love and care and light in the world were leaving me. I crept close to her, meaning to spring secretly onto the shining place and so go away with them, but she spied me and said, "Silly Radulphus, you cannot," and that *you* hurt me more than anything else, so that I began to bawl.

"Child," said the Abbess, "come to me," and loudly weeping I leaned against her knees. I felt the shining around me, all bright and good and warm, that wiped away all grief, and then the Abbess's touch on my hair.

She said, "Remember me. And be . . . content."

I nodded, wishing I dared to look up at her face, but when I did, she had already gone with her friends. Not up into the sky, you understand, but as if they moved very swiftly backwards among the trees—although the trees were still behind them somehow—and as they moved, the shining and the people faded away into the rain until there was nothing left.

Then there was no rain. I do not mean that the clouds parted or the sun came out; I mean that one moment it was raining and cold and the next the sky was clear blue from side to side and it was splendid, sunny, breezy, bright, sailing weather. I had the oddest thought that the strange folk were not agreed about doing such a big miracle—and it was hard for them, too—but they had decided that no one would believe this more than all the other miracles folk speak of, I suppose. And it would surely make Thorvald's lot easier when he came back with wild words about saints and Heaven, as indeed it did, later.

Well, that is the tale, really. She said to me "Be content" and so I am; they call me Radulf the Happy now. I have had my share of trouble and sickness but always somewhere in me there is a little spot of warmth and joy to make it all easier, like a traveler's fire burning out in the wilderness on a cold night. When I am in real sorrow or distress I remember her fingers touching my hair and that takes part of the pain away, somehow. So perhaps I got the best gift, after all. And she said also, "Remember me," and thus I have, every little thing, although it all happened when I was the age my own grandson is now, and that is how I can tell you this tale today.

And the rest? Three days after the Norsemen left, Sibihd got back her wits and no one knew how, though I think I do! And as for Thorvald Einarsson, I have heard that after his wife died in Norway he went to England and ended his days there as a monk, but whether this story be true or not I do not know.

I know this: they may call me Happy Radulf all they like, but there is much that troubles me. Was the Abbess Radegunde a demon, as the new priest says? I cannot believe this, although he called half her sayings nonsense and the other half blasphemy when I asked him. Father Cairbre, before the Norse killed him, told us stories about the Sidhe, that is the Irish fairy people, who leave changelings in human cradles, and for a while it seemed to me that Radegunde must be a woman of the Sidhe when I remembered that she could read Latin at the age of two and was such a marvel of learning when so young, for the change-

lings the fairies leave are not their own children, you understand, but one of the fairy-folk themselves, who are
hundreds upon hundreds of years old, and the other fairy-
folk always come back for their own in the end. And yet this
could not have been, for Father Cairbre said also that the
Sidhe are wanton and cruel and without souls, and neither
the Abbess Radegunde nor the people who came for her
were one blessed bit like that, although she did break Thorfinn's neck—but then it may be that Thorfinn broke his own
neck by chance, just as we all thought at the time, and she
told this to Thorvald afterwards, as if she had done it herself,
only to frighten him. She had more of a soul with a soul's
griefs and joys than most of us, no matter what the new
priest says. He never saw her or felt her sorrow and lone-
someness, or heard her talk of the blazing light all around
us—and what can that be but God Himself? Even though
she did call the crucifix a deaf thing and vain, she must have
meant not Christ, you see, but only the piece of wood itself,
for she was always telling the Sisters that Christ was in
Heaven and not on the wall. And if she said the light was not
good or evil, well, there is a traveling Irish scholar who told
me of a holy Christian monk named Augustinus who tells us
that all which is, is good, and evil is only a lack of the good,
like an empty place not filled up. And if the Abbess truly said
there was no God, I say it was the sin of despair, and even
saints may sin, if only they repent, which I believe she did at
the end.

So I tell myself and yet I know the Abbess Radegunde
was no saint, for are the saints few and weak, as she said?
Surely not! And then there is a thing I held back in my telling, a small thing and it will make you laugh and perhaps
means nothing one way or the other but it is this:

Are the saints bald?

These folk in white had young faces but they were like

eggs; there was not a stitch of hair on their domes! Well, God may shave His saints if He pleases, I suppose.

But I know she was no saint. And then I believe that she did kill Thorfinn and the light was not God and she not even a Christian or maybe even human and I remember how Radegunde was to her only a gown to step out of at will, and how she truly hated and scorned Thorvald until she was happy and safe with her own people. Or perhaps it was like her talk about living in a house with the rooms shut up; when she stopped being Radegunde first one part of her came back and then the other—the joyful part that could not lie or plan and then the angry part—and then they were all together when she was back among her own folk. And then I give up trying to weigh this matter and go back to warm my soul at the little fire she lit in me, that one warm, bright place in the wide and windy dark.

But something troubles me even there, and will not be put to rest by the memory of the Abbess's touch on my hair. As I grow older it troubles me more and more. It was the very last thing she said to me, which I have not told you but will now. When she had given me the gift of contentment, I became so happy that I said, "Abbess, you said you would be revenged on Thorvald, but all you did was change him into a good man. That is no revenge!"

What this saying did to her astonished me, for all the color went out of her face and left it gray. She looked suddenly old, like a death's head, even standing there among her own true folk with love and joy coming from them so strongly that I myself might feel it. She said, "I did not change him. I lent him my eyes; that is all." Then she looked beyond me, as if at our village, at the Norsemen loading their boats with weeping slaves, at all the villages of Germany and England and France where the poor folk sweat from dawn to dark so that the great lords may do battle with one another, at castles under siege with the starving folk within eating mice and rats and sometimes each other, at the women carried off or raped or beaten, at the mothers wailing for their little ones, and beyond this at the great wide world itself with all its battles which I had used to think so grand, and the misery and greediness and fear and jealousy and hatred of folk one for the other, save—perhaps—for a few small bands of savages, but they were so far from us that one could scarcely see them. She said: *No revenge? Thinkest thou so, boy?* And then she said as one who believes absolutely, as one who has seen all the folk at their living and dying, not for one year but for many, not in one place but in all places, as one who knows it all over the whole wide earth:

Think again. . . .

"So that's how the world was saved," said the schoolkid. "By those aliens with their telepathic powers."

"Do you believe that?" said the tutor. "Then you'd believe anything! No, it wasn't like that at all. They went away in the twelfth century A.D. on business of their own and never came back. But there had been some telepathic contagion (perhaps) because many years later . . ."

The Mystery of the Young Gentleman

No sooner had Eliza entered her Dungeon than the first thought which occurred to her, was how to get out of it again.

She went to the Door; but it was locked. She looked at the Window; but it was barred with iron; disappointed in both her expectations, she despaired of effecting her Escape, when she fortunately perceived in the Corner of her Cell, a small saw and a ladder of ropes. . . .

—*HENRY AND ELIZA,* JANE AUSTEN

June 6, 1885—embarking on the S.S. *President Hayes,* London to New York. I have been reading Charcot and chuckling—the things these people manage to invent when they try to explain one another!—but know you will want all the physical science and economic theory you can get and so have sent ahead the proceedings of the Royal Society, the *Astronomical Journal,* recent issues of *The Lancet,* etc. and a very interesting new volume called *Capital,* which I think you will find useful. Maria-Dolores has submitted with decent civility to the necessity of skirts, petticoats, and boots, and luckily for me has discovered in herself a positive liking for bonnets; otherwise only her incapacity for proper English prevents her from the worst excesses of which she's capable. Having a fifteen-year-old from the slums of Barcelona registered as one's daughter is a tricky way to make the passage, especially since I have also my living to earn, as usual. I will continue to write to you in my spare time during the crossing; if this is mailed in New York, it will reach Denver before us. In any event the scribbling can do no harm—I will keep the stuff locked up and can use the practice in this odd skill, though it is no substitute for the real thing, as you and I (in my misery!) both know. It helps keep one's mind off the ship: one huge din only beginning to become separated from the infinitely more vast roar of London itself, which has got almost beyond bearing the last few weeks. I have bought a great many dime novels on which Maria-Dolores can practice her English; if these fail, I will concentrate on her manners, which are abominable. (The last few weeks have been given over entirely to lessons in Eating: Not Reaching, Not Using One's Fingers, Not Swearing, and so on.)

Clatter clatter bang-bang! (Maria-Dolores coming down the companionway. Next will be Walking.)

"*Mamacita!*" (Loudly present in her cabin, which adjoins mine.)

I correct her automatically. "*Papá.*"

She turns red. "*Papá.*" Then, in Spanish, coming in to where I am sitting, writing: "I hate these shoes. I cannot remove them."

I reach into the tiny desk, withdraw the button hook, and show it to her, out of her reach. She says, "But they pain me, *Papá.*" She then instructs her boots, in Spanish, to fuck themselves, whereupon I lock the button hook up again. She is a good little soul and clings to me, half-erotically, pouting: "Papa, may I have dinner with you and the Captain tonight?"

I slap her hand away; she is not to steal the key. I say, "You have twelve years, Maria-Dolores. Behave so."

"*Tu madre!*" says she. I am trying not to feel those wild, bare feet shut up in a London bootmaker's fantasy for little girls. I say in English, "Maria-Dolores, a gentleman cannot travel with a young woman of fifteen, however short and small. Nor can he eat with her until she learns how to behave. Now lie down and read your books. The feet will heal."

"Next time I will be your son," says Maria-Dolores, limping unnecessarily into her cabin. But I see her see *Miner Ned, Stories of the West,* and the others; there is the thrill, the rush, the heart-stopping joy. She thinks: *these* books! and throws herself down on the bed without a pain; I get up and go in to where I have a view of her white-kid calves and her child's dress.

I say, "Maria-Dolores, I am your father and you have forgotten to thank me."

She turns around, baffled. We're alone.

I say, "If you always behave in private as you must in public, then you will never forget the proper behavior in public."

I have put some force into this and she gets up off the bed, her feelings hurt. You understand, much of this is still mysterious to her. She curtseys, as I taught her. "*Gracias, papá.*"

"In English, now," I say.

"Thank you, papa, for the books. I am sure to be pleased with them."

"Good," I say; "Much better. Now read," and instantly she is worlds away, her long black hair hanging over the edge of the bed. What they would make of us at the Salpêtrière!—but luckily Europe is now far enough away to be out of the range of my worry. England also. There is no

extraordinary intelligence on board among the first-class
passengers, although an elderly physician down the corridor
has been observing the two of us from the first hour of
boarding, with an "acute," thoroughly amateurish attention I
find both exasperating and excruciatingly funny. I will have
to keep an eye on him nonetheless; as they say in the mountains, even a goose can walk from Leadville to Kansas, given
enough time. (There are some remarkable minds in steerage
but they are not preoccupied with us.) Joe Smith of Colorado then dresses for dinner: a diamond ring flat-cut, gold
nuggets fastening the shirt-front, a gold watch, solid gold
tobacco-case, the pearl-handled derringer, hair brushed back
from a central parting with the mahogany-backed brushes
Maria-Dolores took such a fancy to in the shop window in
the Rue de Rivoli two weeks ago. Coming out into the corridor I have the very great pleasure of meeting the doctor's
displeasure, so I stop, causing him to stop, roll my own, and
light up. Instantly the dubious Italian with the little mistress
becomes a young Western gentleman: well-off, tall, lean, still
deeply sun-burnt. One must be careful, speaking: it's too
easy to answer questions that haven't been asked. I say only,
"Good evening, Doctor."

"How—"

I smile. "I overheard you speaking to another pas-
senger. Not voluntary on my part, I assure you. And if I may
take the liberty of answering the inevitable question, the accent is what you fellows call 'mid-Atlantic.' I was educated
at ———."

His university, his college. We talk about that. He's
looking for flaws but of course finds none. He bumbles a bit
(rather obviously) about "the young lady" but when I swear
and say she's an awful nuisance, makes me feel desperately
awkward, needs a woman's care, unexpected wardship, aunt
in Denver, second cousin fiancée, so on, it's all right. There
is, in all this, a strong pull towards me and I wonder for a

moment if there's going to be real trouble, but it's only the
usual confusion and mess. We are chatting. I think I have
located the poker game. The doctor asks me to dine with
him and I assent, would look odd not to. He takes a deep
breath and pushes out his chest, saying authoritatively, "It
will be a mild crossing." This is to impress me. At table are
two married women, temporarily husbandless, whom I try
to stay away from, an old man absorbed in his debts and the
ruin of his business, and a mother-daughter pair of that help-
less-hopeless kind in which enforced misery breeds enforced hatred, all this made by the locking together, the real
need of one for the other. There is an enormous amount of
plumes, flounces, pillowings, corsets, tight boots. (Maria-
Dolores, stealing rabbits, was luckier.) There are cut flowers
at the center of the table (the first night), too much food,
heavy monogrammed glasses, heavy monogrammed cutlery
and china, and a vague, generalized appreciation of all this
that is not pleasure but a kind of abstract sense of gratification. (Look up "wealth.") Everything coarsened and sim-
plified for reasons of commerciality and the possibility of
rough weather. No one notices the waiter (who is a union
organizer). I make my escape after dinner but only to an
interlude with the younger of the married women. We are
all charming—you, I, Maria-Dolores—we have to be, we
can't turn off; and in this situation and class there are ap-
proaches to which a gentleman must give in, despite the
rules. ("What a beautiful night, Mr. Smith. Do you like
stars?") She can't go anywhere in the evening without a
companion. So we walk doggedly round and round the
deck, Mrs. ———— making most of the conversation—"So
you own a silver mine in Leadville, Mr. Smith?" "My father
does, ma'am"—until that topic gives out. Maria-Dolores is a
bad excuse for leaving, as Mrs. ———— will "take an interest"
in and want to "form" her. That dull, perpetual, coerced lack
she has been taught to call "love," which a gentleman's arm,

a gentleman's face, a gentleman's conversation, so wonderfully soothes. It's a deadly business. I get away, finally, to the
poker game in the gentlemen's lounge—that is, one of the
gentlemen's lounges—where the problem is not to win but
to keep from winning too much. I always lose, as a matter of
rule, on the first night.

"A new man! What's your name?"

"Joseph Smith, Colorado."

Unoriginal jokes about Mormons, lots of nervous laughter, bragging, forceful shaking of hands. Then they talk about
women. No one over thirty but one older professional I'm
going to have to watch out for. I allow a bit of Leadville in
my speech, what they expect: Not playing with you folks, of
course, just thought I'd watch.

The serious game. The fear of death, of failure. Risking
fate, surviving it. One leaves, secretly in tears, saying casu-
ally "I'm cleaned out." I balance what I see, what I "should"
see, what they think I see. It's a hot little room. I lose a little,
win a little more, then lose again, then drop pretty cata-
strophically, more than three hundred pounds.

"You'll want to get that back," says the professional,
who's clever enough to know I'm no novice. He's also been
marking the deck, which makes things easier. I lose again—
some—and he lets me win back about a third. Winks: "Quit
while you're ahead." I go on and lose again. Which is time to
leave, mentioning the rich dad and his moral objections.

"I thought you fellows were born with a deck of cards
in your hands!"

A promise—(embarrassed).

"What's wrong with a bit of fun?" (pretending to be
aggrieved).

He says, confident, "See you tomorrow night."

So that's done. Maria-Dolores is asleep. Old Doctor
Bumble passes me in the hall, beams and bows, delighted,
unaware that his young friend is going to the dogs. I unlock

the door to my stateroom, waking Maria-Dolores, who calls, "Come talk to me." This means exactly what it says: I'm lonely, I'm curious, I like you, I want a little chat. She is, like most of us at that age, surprisingly transparent.

She says honestly, "Papá, what makes the ship go?"

"Engines," I say. "Great big ones. Down there." (Pointing to the floor.) "They burn coal."

"At night, too?" Amusing to see her trying to imagine this phenomenon; she knows only a coal stove.

"Men shovel coal into them," I say. "All night long."

She wakes up. "*Now?*"

"Yes, right now."

A vivid picture in her mind of a vast cave with doors about it and flame within. "It must be exciting."

"Not to them," I say.

She is surprised.

"Because," I say, to answer her, "it's very hot. And very, very hard. And they want badly to sleep."

She tries to think why they do it and then solves the puzzle: "If they make the ship go, they decide where it goes."

"No," I say. "Someone else. Not the Captain, the Board of Directors— No, not wood. Men."

She thinks sleepily, embroidering the furnace room (which I can see, hear, smell, touch from a dozen vantages) into Aladdin's cave, "They are paid *very* well. They are making their fortunes."

"Later," I say. She can join the argument about how much to help the others after we get home. The answer is in the books she has been reading, but books don't count; they aren't real. Only Barcelona has poor people. And even Barcelona has been kind to orphaned Maria-Dolores. Not like scowling, skinny Maria-Elena, who worked sixteen hours a day making matches and lost the feeling in her hands, or pretty, frightened Maria-Teresa, sold and pregnant at thir-

teen, or ugly, hungry, limping Maria-Mercedes with the
sores on her face, whose mamà beat her. Half the little girls
in the Spanish slums are named after the Virgin; their twin-
kling, bare legs run like mice in Maria-Dolores's dreams.
Asleep now. Something has always protected this mouse,
warned her, led her, warmed her. Something has kept her
safe and happy, even at fifteen.

Like you. Like me.

June 7—An arch note from Mrs. ———, so I become
ill, stay in the cabin in my dressing gown all day, and drill
Maria-Dolores in manners. She gets madder and madder and
towards evening begins to pester me:

"Next time I travel as your son!"

Once we get into the mountains, I tell her, she can
travel as anything she likes. Even a hoppy-toad.

"I want *that*"—picture in a book of a young lady in full
sail. Can she dress like that when we get home? Part of this
is merely for nuisance's sake, but she is really fed up with
being a twelve-year-old. I say yes, we'll send to Denver for
it.

"Well, can I dress like a man?"

"Like this?" (pointing to myself) "Of course."

She says, being a real pest, "I bet there are no women in
the mountains."

"That's right," I tell her. (She's also in real confusion.)

"But *me!*" she says.

"When you get there, there will still be no women."

"But you— Is it all *men?*"

"There are no men. Maria-Dolores, we've been over and
over this."

She gives up, exasperated. Her head, like all the others',
is full of *los hombres y las mujeres* as if it were a fact of
nature: ladies with behinds inflated as if by bicycle pumps,
gentlemen with handlebar mustachios who kiss the ladies'

hands. If I say *las hombres y los mujeres,* as I once did and am tempted to do again, she will kick me.

"I'm bored!" She wanders to the porthole, looks out, reflecting that there's nothing interesting out there, and a whole world of people on the ship, but I am keeping her away from them.

There's something more. I have, I think, been lying to myself, as is so easy out here; she's too old; we have been together too long. I have been as cold to her as I dared, fearing this. I turn my back, put on my dinner jacket, tie my tie; she raises her eyes. An electric shock, an unbearable temptation. As when things rush together in a new form in someone's mind. Oh my dear, what will I do? What will I say? This is a real human being; this is one of ours.

She says, "You know everything. So why even ask? I've done it before. With girls, too; girls do it with girls and boys with boys; everybody knows that."

She gets out softly, after a moment's struggle, "I like you."

I say, without expression, "Close the outer door." When she has: "Sit down. No, no, on the other side of the room." Then:

"You are thinking how nice it would be, aren't you? You are thinking of it right now."

The resulting wave almost knocks me over. I continue as if it had not happened: "No. It would not be nice at all.

"Look, Maria-Dolores, we have talked about this before, about the difference and how, when you are a baby, you shut it off. Well, it isn't something you can choose to turn on or off, as you close or open your eyes. One loses one's sense of oneself at first; it is like being hammered to death. With so much clamor all around you, either you will shut again so fast that nothing will ever get you open or you will go crazy, like a mouse shut up in clockwork, and I must get doctors to put you to sleep with morphia for weeks to come—and this is bad for your health and very expensive and worst of all it will bring a great deal of suspicion down on me, which neither of us can afford. Do you want them to take you away from me and shut you up somewhere forever?" (Or all the other things!)

Well, she has been following this, but she has also been taking considerable pleasure in watching my lips move; I have to hold on rather hard to the writing desk. She says, "But why—" and then stops, understanding finally that I know. "Because," I say, "this is how it happens when one is young," and knowing so much more than she, sit down, knees giving away, with my face in my hands. The two mirrors so placed that they reflect each other to infinity, as you see in a barbershop, each knowing what the other feels. That remembered fusion which opens everything, even minds. So lost that I literally do not know she has crossed the little cabin until I hear her breathing. I smelled her hair and body before I saw her. She says, "Can we do it later?" and I nod. Somewhere in Kansas, miles from anyone! She says, very moved, "Oh, give me one kiss to show you don't hate me!" and I manage to say, "I don't hate you, Maria-Dolores, leave me alone, please," but cannot any longer trust myself with the act of speaking. She's planning to kiss me, little liar, and after that it will be really impossible, a wonderful impossible whirling descent from which I really cannot move. But manage to get up somehow and out into the corridor without touching her—fatal!—and the door shut and locked, which helps, as you would expect, not at all. So I did deliberately what I last did involuntarily fifteen years ago, confronted with my first town (three hundred souls) and no matter that old Bumble is ambling around the bend of the corridor: first things first.

Shut it all out.

The smell of orange blossoms, which becomes pungent

and choking: sal ammoniac. Bumble withdraws, turning his back on me. I'm lying on something, not in my own cabin, and for a blurred moment can't see anything of him but his broad back. As helpless as any of them. He says, "I thought it best not to alarm the young lady."

I find myself coughing uncontrollably, sitting up on the edge of his berth, bed, what-do-you-call-it. I'm awake. He really is extraordinarily stupid. He says, "You seem to have cracked a rib." Having had, you understand, perhaps ninety seconds to get his first really good look at me, he has put two and two together and got five: *Uranian. Invert. Onanist.* (These are words they make up; you will find them in medical texts.) It may surprise you that this kind of thing does not happen often, but the division is so strong, so elaborate, so absolute, so much trained into them as habit, that within reasonable limits they see, generally, more or less what they expect to see, especially if one wears the mask of the proper behavior. His mistake has been made before, but those who make it usually do not speak out, either from the concern of fellowship or simply lack of interest. This one is that fatal combination: kindness and curiosity. For under the surface indignation he is pitying and embarrassed and would really like to say, Look here, dear fellow, let's forget all this, pretend it never happened, eh? and we'll both be so much happier. But he is fascinated, too. He is even, unknown to himself, attracted. He has, you see, the genuine fixing on the female body, but there is also its dirtiness, its repulsiveness, its profound fearfulness, which as a doctor he must both acknowledge and feel more strongly (and believes, because he is a doctor, that his confusions have the status of absolute truth), and then, worst of all, there is the terrible dullness of the business, which comes with the half-disillusionment of old age: women, the silliness of women, the perpetual disappointments of the act (no wonder!), the uncleanliness of the whole business, and finally the sullying and base suspicion that it's merely "propagation," one of the nasty cheats of an impersonal and soulless Nature, unless one is fool enough to sentimentalize it. (He sums all this up by saying from time to time, "I'm too old for all that; let the young men make fools of themselves!")

He harrumphs. Bumbles. Fudges. Peeks at me. Out of the welter comes:

"You—you ought to have that rib looked at, you know." (Thinks of himself investigating under the taping, greedy old pussycat!)

I say, "Thank you, I have. Immobility's not the thing, I'm told."

"Accident?"

"No, fight." He thinks he knows about what. He tiptoes about me mentally with all the elaborate skill of old Rutherford B. Hayes trying to catch a squirrel, fumbling with the tools in his medical bag as if he had something else to put back there, coughing, arranging and rearranging his stethoscope—and there is such a resemblance between the two that I cannot forbear imagining the doctor caught under the corner of our front porch at home and having to be pulled out yowling, his tail lashing, his fur erect, his sense of autonomy irretrievably shattered, and pieces of dust and cobweb stuck on his elderly ginger whiskers (which they both have). He says:

"You ought to . . . lead a more active life. Open-air exercise, you know. Build yourself up."

I say, "I live on a ranch, Doctor."

He bursts out, "But my dear fellow, you mustn't— it is quite obvious— you owe it to your father—and that poor child—"

I say dryly, "She is a good deal safer with me than with you, surely." This is calculated to enrage him. I admit the logic of the matter is hard to follow, but at its base you will find a remarkable confusion of ideas: heredity, biological causation, illness, choice, moral contamination, and some five or six other notions that have not quite got settled. There is also the backhanded compliment to the virility of a man of sixty. Why does old Rutherford B. Hayes, an hour after his ignominious handling by one of us, dimly convince himself that he has been rescued by an adorer and leap to one's bosom in gratitude, demanding liver? The cases are not unlike. Bumble is not only stupid, as I have said, but his stupidity is actually the principal cause of his kindliness. I don't mean this as cruelly as it sounds; let's say only that he has a genuine innocence, something fresh that his "ideas" don't affect, still less his "decency," which is (as is usual with them) the worst thing about him. My remark takes a moment to activate the mechanism; then drawing himself up—for I ought to have the "decency" to be disgusted at myself, that's the worst of it—he levels the most damning accusation he can, poor old soul: "Damn it, sir, you know what you are!"

Let him stew a bit. I re-stud my shirt, slowly, and fasten the cuffs, feel for my tie. Adjust the artfully tailored dinner jacket. I have come out without the derringer, or Bumble would remember it and he doesn't. What would he have made of it? He is beginning to be ashamed of himself, so now is the time to speak. I say steadily:

"Doctor, I am what my nature has made me. It was not my choice and I deserve neither blame nor credit in the business. I have done nothing in the whole of my life of which I need be ashamed, and I hope you will pardon me if I observe that, in my case, that has been of necessity a much lonelier and more bitter business than it has in yours." Here I take from his bedside stand the elaborately gold-framed photograph of his dead wife, saying, "I assume, sir, that this lady is some near kin to you?"

He nods, already remorseful. Says gruffly, "My wife."

I put it down. "Children?"

He nods. "Grown now, of course." Better to leave the comparison unspoken. I merely say, "You may be sure, sir, that my little Spanish cousin is as morally safe with me as if she were in church. A married sister of mine in Denver wishes to give her a home. That is where I am taking her."

Not too thick. Leave quickly. We talk a bit more, about my sister, one Mrs. Butte, and the nieces and nephews—his preconceived notions of what the family is like are a trouble to me as they're rather strong and I have to work some not to match him too closely—and by then he is so pleased with himself for having been so very generous and good— and so lucky, too, in comparison with you-know-who—that he offers me a drink. I say:

"No, sir. I am no abstainer; I take wine with my dinner, as you have seen, but otherwise I do not indulge."

He pooh-poohs.

I shake my head. "Not hard liquor, Doctor. Our frontier offers too many bad examples. In the mining camps I have seen so many ruined that way—good, normal young fellows whom I envied. Those tragedies have helped to keep me straight. What is only a temptation to you is poison to me, sir."

He says, solicitous, "But the pain of that rib—"

I shake my head.

He's very moved.

So am I.

Then off to the poker game, with a poker face, to win back two hundred and fifty pounds. This is how it's done: Lose spectacularly but win little by little, and pocket some from time to time so that you don't seem to have won too much. This takes only a very moderate sleight-of-hand when others' attention is elsewhere.

But the card sharp knows.

June 9—Two days' bad weather, seasickness, almost all

the passengers down. To avoid puking my guts out because of the bombardment of others' misery, I must mesmerize myself more lightly than for sleep, but heavily enough to put everything into a comfortable, drunken blur. (In this condition, the novels I have bought for Maria-Dolores actually make a kind of sense.) That young lady, unaffected, eating heartily and in an ecstasy of freedom, is running alone about the almost unpeopled first-class deck and dining room. The list of rules: Not to speak or understand English, swear, take her boots off, show her bottom, make obscene gestures, go anywhere but first class, and so on. She laughed, hearing it. Someone's saying authoritatively—somewhere in the ship— that the weather will let up tomorrow; we are skirting the edge of something-or-other. But I did not catch most of it.

June 10—That old tomcat has been *writing up my case,* as he calls it: names, dates, details, everything that must never get into print! He even plans to bribe the steward to find out if there are women's clothes in my steamer trunk, a piece of idiocy that will land us both in an instant mess. I've explained to Maria-Dolores, who merely shrugged, bored to death, poor soul, and violently moody from having to restrain her feelings about me. She says, "Go tear it up."

"No," I say, "*he* must tear it up. Otherwise"— and I point significantly to the porthole.

She remarks that he is probably too fat to go through, opining that the English are all mad anyway. Her judgment of *maricons* is that (a) they're all over the place and (b) who cares (a view to which I certainly wish the good doctor would subscribe) and (c) please, please, please, can she go outside if only for a little before she goes mad herself?

"Yes," I say, "Yes, now you must." She whoops into the other room. For I know how—now—and will tell her, although like Mrs. H. B. Carrington, whose *Mystery of the*

Stolen Bride (8 vo., boards, illus.) Maria-Dolores is now about to fling out the porthole she has got open—I have to shout "Stop that at once!"—I won't tell you. They never do in their books; that makes the story more lifelike for them, I suppose. So you may pretend you are one of them now, and don't skip.

I'm going to brand him. So badly that he will never write a word about me—or want to think it, either. I think you can guess. Not nice, but easier than drowning, and safer (in these crowds).

Now he is writing in a burst of inspiration—this very minute—that the only influence that has saved me from the "fate" of my "type" (lace stockings, female dress, self-pollution, frequenting low haunts, unnatural acts, drunkenness, a love of cosmetics, inevitable moral degeneration, eventual insanity, it goes on for pages, it is really the most dreadful stuff) *is my healthy outdoor life in the manly climate of the American West!*

Maria-Dolores has just popped her head in to know why I'm laughing so hard. Memories of the mining camps, I tell her. Bumble, you deserve it, you deserve it all.

After much thought, he proudly puts down the title: "A Hitherto Unconsidered Possibility: The Moral Invert."

June 14—First class is commodes and red plush everywhere. A new dress every day. The moral fogginess, bad enough here, takes a sharp rise two levels down—out of simple desperation—then drops to something approaching limited realism as you enter steerage. (Not that anyone really sees much more than one rung above or below them on the ladder; the rest fades into mist.) Afternoons Mrs. ———, the doctor, and I make up a party with Maria-Dolores as its supposed center; at dinner, Maria-Dolores gone, everyone eats uncontrollably (as they've been doing all day), and Mrs. ———, flushed with the day's victories, makes a very determined set at me over the wine. I dodge. Bumble, outwardly approving, nonetheless manages always to claim his young friend for the evening somehow, and then the two of us spend the next few hours in little secret orgies of sentimentality by the rail, watching the stars: "My dear fellow, a lovely woman like that!"—"But, Doctor, how can I honestly—and married—" Well, he didn't mean. He didn't really. Smokes. Sighs. Points out constellations. Discusses God. His substitute for emotion (all on Mrs. ———'s account, mind you). Not that any young fellow would arouse anything but wrath by attacking Bumble on the surface, as it were. But slowly, solemnly, he asks. Solemnly, tragic and shamed, I answer. And slowly, slowly, I begin to talk *at* him, as one may say, smoke *at* him, look *at* him, from the turn of the head to the smile, to the slouch, the drawl, the hands in the pockets, until one of us would know—even stone blind—what is going on. Bumble, who is not one of us—he has not a trace of the pattern—doesn't, though it's all tailored to him. From him: suppressed memories of secondary school, memories of his wife. We have been staying up later and later, which cuts into my time at cards, so I sleep later and later but never too late for the all-important staying in shape—Maria-Dolores, at my ever-sleepier push-ups and workings-out: "Ugh. What *for?*"

Later: five-card draw. If you want the technical details, look about you; I've been at it too long to consider them anything but a complete bore. The company, somewhat reduced by now, is made up largely of young men, very free and easy in their manners but in fact deferring markedly to what I will call The Old Fake, the grizzled old professional with muttonchop whiskers, the usual rank-and-hierarchy business, so it will be no hard matter to shift their allegiance if only I can get the other things to work right. Having eaten all day, they now eat more; food and drink arriving periodically, bringing nothing useful to me but a little fresh air. One's lungs are at risk.

I come in late, nod, sit down. The O.F., who has an arrangement with one of the waiters, calls for an unopened deck, which is brought in with more food, more whiskey, all in amounts I haven't the heart to describe. (There is, especially, a tray of bratwurst that is almost enough to propel one out of the room.)

T.O.F.: "Mr. Smith doesn't indulge?"

Someone makes a joke about Mrs. ————.

At this one just smiles; that's best.

Play. More play. We go on, everyone smoking ferociously. The deck is marked. The Old Fake is being careful not to win too openly, so when he decides not to take a hand, I (if at all possible) do. It's a great convenience. It also begins to look uncanny, which is good.

Nobody wants to comment, because you know what *that* means. T.O.F., understanding that I've broken his code, drops back cautiously.

I make a pile.

Then Fake, outwardly grinning, suggests that we switch our games, poker to women; the waiter can bring anything. (He does have it arranged; there are women who work this crossing, as in every other.)

I say that when I play cards, playing cards is what I do.

Now the hardest thing in the world is to wait for something that will make you look surprised. T.O.F.—he's fifty-five and all he's done for the last twenty years is eat and sit—keeps me staring at the table-top an unconscionable, trying time. Then he says that of course Mr. Smith doesn't crave the new game; he has all he wants of that without paying for it.

Then he makes a joke about Maria-Dolores.

Well, I can't turn pale, of course, but there's a reason-able-looking way to impersonate the effect of this, done mostly with muscles and a fixed gaze, so that's what I do. I get up slowly and slowly I draw—no, not the derringer, not tonight; someone might, after all, get hold of it—but the Bowie (shoulder holster) and the room goes electric.

I say slowly, *turning pale,* "Why, you God-damned skunk!"

Then the knife, extremely sharp point first, driven deep into the polished surface of the table—see, I won't use it!— all very stupid and out of the kind of thriller you-know-who spends her nights reading. T.O.F., across the table from me, seated almost against the wall, rises, expecting that I'll circle—he's worried and planning to back off, protesting he meant no harm—but it's easy, you see, when you're aware what the other's going to do before he does it. Even before he knows it. The table's bolted to the floor and is pretty solid, too, so one can vault over it as over a fence, using one arm as a lever, and skidding a bit, really, feet first into poor Fake, that tub of lard (they all get like that at his age), staggering the poor old thing crash! against the wall. Then a couple of punches for show; he's had the wind knocked out of him already.

(And that, child, is *why.* She once poked my chest and said "But how do you breathe?" Me: "From my belly, like you.")

Breathing a little hard—no, it's *not* enough, even for one raised at eleven thousand feet—and getting up into the marvelous scandal:

"Gentlemen, this deck is marked."

Now, that is serious. I say to one of the young 'uns, "Jones, pick a card." And call it. And again. And again. And then again. Several begin, aghast, "But—" with a mental sniff-and-point at T.O.F., whom I now leave prudently on his side of the table. (And how much will damaging the furniture add to tonight's bill? Oh, Lord!)

I say, "Who ordered the deck?"

Turmoil. Nobody's sure. One bursts out: "But I did! I asked Mr.———" (follows hand-over-mouth and he *does* turn pale).

Now everyone believes. Sensation. Thrill. Real horror. These are their "standards." This is their "code." I say, spreading out what I've won, "Gentlemen, if you remember your losses . . . ?

"This has been no fair game," I say, "and I have no taste for further play," and go out leaving a great deal of money and a lot of conflicting feelings behind me, the latter being the direct result of the former. (Let them straighten it out.)

So now *I* am head faker. You see? And can stretch my luck a little for the next few nights. I will clear, I think, some two thousand pounds before we land, with luck.

What a species.

Still, even blind—!

June 15—This is how it happens:

A fine, balmy night, the doctor standing at the rail smoking his cigar and looking out over the sea. I'm facing him, having rolled a cigarette (no anatomical comparisons, please!): two friends under the stars. Time is pressing and the doctor very uneasy. He wants to be away from the lights, so the women who drift slowly past, in pairs or accompanied by gentlemen, are recognizable only in silhouette, the dim shape of sleeves and skirt, the massed hair and hat, the gleam of an earring. The doctor is at sea and memories are disturbing him, all the more that he's not quite sure what they are. He's also a little drunk. We've been talking ever more confidentially: his school days, his friends, then the past few days on shipboard, then his wife, their meeting, our meeting, our talks, until all have fallen together in confusion; he feels the same nostalgia for all of them. He finds this troubling. Finally I lean closer, for all must happen under water now, dream-slow, dream-fast, and I say, somehow too close although still barely half-seen, hands in pockets, leaning against the rail, a low voice out of the darkness:

Bumble, your companionship and your example have meant a great deal to me these past few days.

The slight stammer excites him, the slouch, the soft, precise wording, the lifted chin. All memorable, all unidentifiable. He mutters something self-deprecatory and turns to leave, extremely uncomfortable, but I'm in his way, looking more like *it* than ever. It says:

I cannot say, Doctor, how much I admire you, how much I look up to you.

He protests.

It says: *I would put this in stronger terms, but there's no need. Surely you know.*

Bumble begins to drown. I am close enough to take his arm now or he would bolt; he feels the grip and the heat through his clothes, almost as if they were gone; almost, his hand is being held. *It* says, a disembodied voice, a hard, hot touch on his arm—and this time there is warm breath on his neck—

As you told me yourself, there is an instinct in such things which can never be mistaken.

In a moment he'll go under; mermaids will tickle his ears with streams of bubbles: Who am I? Do I remind you of someone? They'll be playing with his hair, tweaking his ears. He'll be picked bones in a moment. The cylindrical people, the flounced-and-puffed people, pass by, a world away.

It says in his wife's voice, with the odd, light break between the syllables, which he feels as the tip of a tongue: *Ed-ward . . . ?*

Bumble is pulling at my arm. He's in a panic. He's about to drop his cigar and top hat and won't know it. They can't stand two kinds of knowledge that don't mix—not knowing the secret—but then he finds the way out for himself and I wish you could see it—even Bumble!—like a switchback on a train ride: jerk! jerk! jerk! and the new track is there, shiny and straight, as convinced as if I had said it myself.

"You're a woman!"

I do nothing. I say nothing. I don't have to, you see, I have only to smile, all sex in my smile. He will do it all himself, from "My dear girl, why didn't you tell me!" to "But you mustn't walk alone, oh dear, no, you mustn't go alone to your cabin!" He remembers my face on a playbill (though the name eludes him)—must be an actress, of course, have to be an actress; we have to learn such things for the stage, don't we? Special dress, altered voice, dye on the skin—but nothing injurious, he hopes, nothing that will mar, eh? Don't want to spoil that complexion, not when one needs it for one's work, not when one's famous for it (still searching). And what a clever little woman, to pull it off, when otherwise they'd be all about me, spoiling my trip with their interviews and their publicity.

He babbles: *He* knew. Doctors *know,* you know. Little hands, little feet, smooth face, delicate features, slender body! Quite obvious. Quite, quite obvious. Trying to remember what he said to the gentleman that he oughtn't to have said to the lady—but actresses are different, don't you know—free-thinking—though nothing indelicate—and he was only playing along, you understand, being a little free in his language, but nothing sensible, only gabble, only a lot of nonsense—

In my cabin, not quite remembering how he got there, it all happened so fast. Another drink. He remembers kissing my hands in the corridor. He's in the one armless chair, drink in hand, skittish, embarrassed, giddy with relief and desire, all the dizzy recklessness of a man just made it off a collapsing bridge—when suddenly the little actress is straddling his knees, facing him (a position which would strike him as queer if he were sober) but her face close enough to kiss. Which he does.

I whisper in his ear, "Dear Edward. Dearest, dearest Edward!"

He tries greedily to get at my jacket buttons and can't; I have placed his arms outside mine, behind my back, the two boiled shirt-fronts crackling like armor-plate between us. He tries to get up and so I give him another kiss, a slow one with biting in it. The position bothers him but it's what I need, so I whisper, "Not yet. Let me," and reaching down, undo, to his indescribable shock and utter, helpless delight, the buttons of his trousers. Actresses *are* different. I fish for and play with his pretty thing and kiss his neck and mouth and tell him about the female form divine, which he will see in just a moment: the cushioned hips and swelling bosom and buttocks, and secret, round, moist parts, all the upholstery that stiffens him and makes him push and pant. The liquor's slowing him but it also makes things possible, I mean the doubleness of dreams: right words, wrong smells (tobacco, men's hair-pomade), the armor between us, the lingering confusion about who's who, the sudden reasonless satisfaction with a stranger who knows exactly what fondling he wants, and the magic shameful words his wife never knew, and handles his secret self, as she never would, or put her tongue in his ear, an appalling, hideously exciting novelty. So he abandons himself to the dream, poor silky old sweet tom, which is suddenly happening much too soon— and straining me close and rigid (but my arms are in the way), he heroically tries to stop, I whisper "Shoot me!" and he spends himself freely over my hands and my second-best pair of evening trousers. For a moment he comes back to himself to see his wife—no, the Colorado gambler—no, the actress—in one dim, ambiguous person. He dozes.

He sits, snoring, trousers open. Poor old animal. Maria-Dolores stirs in her next-door sleep. Then, through Bumble's dreaming rag-bag of a mind, goes the overpowering glory of telling the whole story from start to finish: wonders, admirations, successes. He'll do it. He's incorrigible. And will wake up and want more—later tonight, tomorrow night, and so there's nothing else for it. I harden my heart.

He wakes. What is the dear girl doing?

I am, having washed my hands, sitting at my writing desk cleaning a Smith and Wesson forty-five, with canvas over the desk-top to protect it. Also hides the Bowie. The doctor says gruffly, to an unidentifiable back, tears in his eyes: "So you fancied the old fellow, eh?"

Then, "My dear, couldn't you—that is, we're alone—something more natural?"

I say, without turning round, "It's all costume."

He chuckles. "Jewelry!" he says archly (the shirt studs, the diamond).

I say, "They're worth money. I don't collect pound notes for the sound the paper makes, either."

Then I add, "Do you know, I'm quite sure that someone saw us in the corridor."

He can't remember. I say, "You were kissing my hands." He chuckles again, turning red. Hands! He says, "My dear, if you'd only turn—" So I do and he sees what I'm doing. Very puzzling, but there is some good reason, no doubt. I say:

"Doctor, have you read Krafft-Ebing's *Psychopathia Sexualis?*"

He hasn't. He's blank.

"The German medical specialist," I say, "is less generous then you in his view of the male invert. He writes that such people have no morality; they wish only to possess the generative organ of another man by any means, fair or foul; it is their sole object; and they take delight in spreading the contagion of their moral disease, especially when they find the germs of it hidden in an apparently normal man."

No connection. Bumble is slow.

I say, "The German specialist is correct, Doctor. There is, as you yourself told me, an instinct in such matters that

warns against contagion—if we desire to be warned. You,
for example, did not desire to be warned."

Have you ever seen a man turn really pale? The color
goes like a dropped window-shade; it's most impressive. But
the old creature is admirable, in his way; even buttoning his
pants (an act not usually considered dignified among them)
he can give a good impersonation of choleric indignation:
"Sir—I will—I will expose—"

I say evenly, "In that case your own behavior will
hardly bear examination. Remember, we were seen."

"You lied!" he cries, desperate and sincere.

"Did I?" (and I feel for the knife, just in case Bumble
decides to try some first-hand research on my person).
"Why, I don't remember that. What I do remember is saying
nothing at all while you made the whole story up yourself;
you seemed very eager to believe it. An actress? Half a head
taller than yourself? Where in Europe, on what possible
stage? And this business of dye for the skin—which doesn't
smell, won't wash off, and can't be detected even in the
most intimate contact, not even by a medical man? Come!
You lied because you wanted to. And you're lying still."

I add, more softly, "Don't make me dislike you." And
then, in *its* voice, "Keep my secret and I'll keep yours, eh?"

Bumble will launch. Bumble has to be stopped by the
sight of the Bowie, better than the heel of my hand under
his chin and so on. Then Bumble has his inspiration; I did
not lie. I was telling the truth, but I am lying *now.* Reasons?
None at all, but he says flatly, folding his trembling arms
across his chest to indicate unshakable belief:

"You are a woman."

The stupidity. The absolute unconquerable stupidity!
Like the best swordsman in the world beaten by a jackass. I
walk round him, searching, to Maria-Dolores's door. Say,
"Have you heard what happened at cards last night? Yes,
that's me; that is how I get my living; the nonsense about

Colorado helps. Well, I knocked down a man fifty pounds heavier than myself; ask about it tomorrow."

Bumble is trembling.

I turn and flip the knife point-first across the cabin and into the door to the corridor—why is it that acts of manliness always involve damage to the furniture?—which is, you must understand, *something a woman cannot do.* That's faith. I repeat: What a woman cannot do.

Logic also. I say:

"If I am lying now, what is the purpose of my lie? To drive you away? The little actress would not want to drive you away, not after having gone to all the trouble of acquiring you! Why confess she's a woman unless she wanted you? And why should I lie? For fear you'll expose me? I can expose you. I could blackmail you if I wanted; we were seen, you know. To drive you away? I don't want to; I like you—although I don't fancy being attacked and having to knock you down or throttle you as I did to the other gentleman at the game last night—and why on earth, if I wanted to drive you away, should I have taken such trouble to—well, we won't name it. But it's perfect nonsense, my dear fellow, a woman pretending to be a man who pretends he's a woman in order to pretend to be a man? Come, come, it won't work! A female invert might want to dress and live as a man, but to confess she's a woman—which would defeat her purpose—and then be intimate with you—which she would find impossibly repulsive—in order to do what, for heaven's sake? Where's the sense to it? No, there's only one possibility, and that's the truth: that I have been deceiving nobody, including you, but that you, my poor dear fellow, have been for a very long time deceiving yourself. Why not stop, eh? Right now?"

And with a smile, I touch my fingertips to the stain beginning to dry on the front of my trousers and put the fingers in my mouth. Havoc indescribable. This is not nice, not nice at all. If only Bumble does not drop dead this minute, in which case, Maria-Dolores—who has just come in, in her nightgown—and I must put him through the porthole anyhow.

She sees us, imitates alarm, and darts behind the door. Her head peeps out.

Poor grey old man whispers, "Child, has this man ever— has he ever—"

"Maria-Dolores," I say, "this man wants to know if I have ever kissed or touched you. Tell him the truth."

She knows, of course. She says dubiously, "You kiss me good night on the forehead."

"Have I touched you?"

She nods reluctantly, troubled. "You *push* me."

"Push?" says Bumble, grasping at straws.

"When uncle is reading at his desk or busy," says Maria-Dolores, "he *push* me. On the shoulder. He say, 'Go away.' It make me sad. It's happen many time."

Bumble says, "Your uncle—is—is—is he—"

She watches unblinking, as if it were a perfectly normal occurrence for strange old men to twitch and stammer in my cabin long past midnight. I say:

"This gentleman, for reasons I shall not explain to you, wants to know something about me. He wants to know whether I am a man or a woman. Tell him."

She does incredulous surprise much better than I do. Bumble, distressingly, starts to speak; I cut him short: "Not my clothes, Maria-Dolores, and not my behavior. He wants to know the rest of it. Do you understand me? He wants to know what's under the clothes. Tell him you're as ignorant as you ought to be, and you can go back to bed."

She droops, barely audible, "You'll get vexed."

I assure her that I won't.

She says quickly, ashamed and starting to cry, "I did not know. I thought you were away so I came in. You were in the bath they bring in. I ran right out. I will never do it again!"

"Child," says Bumble, "I am sorry to—I don't wish—"

"*Es muy hombre,*" says Maria-Dolores, with a sketchy gesture at her crotch, and by some miracle of acting manages to turn bright red. She adds, looking very embarrassed, "Yes, is a man."

"But do you know," says Bumble unexpectedly coherent, "what a man *is,* child? Do you truly know?"

"Yes, of course," says Maria-Dolores in genuine surprise. Then she looks interested. "Why? Don't you?"

Back to his cabin in a hurry to vomit into the commode, tear up his notes and essay, and burn the pieces in the washbasin.

So that's done.

June 16—Somewhere west of Denver we'll camp for the night, miles from anyone. There in the high country, under the splendid million stars, I'll let down her black hair. Maria-Dolores giggles; she's done it with girls, too. "Joe Smith" of "Colorado" slides his hands under the little girl's shirt—a process I'm sure he could describe very well—but his face will never be reflected in her eyes. She shivers, partly from the cold, whispers, "I want to do things for you, too." I smile Yes, remembering Joe-Bob's lion silkiness and the first surprise of your wiry hair. As I bend slowly down to the nubbiness, the softness, the mossy slipperiness, the heat, that familiar reflection begins back and forth between us, a sudden scatter-shot along the nerves, its focusing on the one place, the echoes in neck and palms and lips, the soles of her feet, her breasts. Maria-Dolores is breathless; "Don't stop!" forgetting that I know. She closes her eyes, sobs, grabs inside, clutches my head with her hand: overwhelming! And sees me, all I remember, all I feel, all I know: overwhelming! And then, out of the things I know—and can't help knowing—she sees the one thing as strange and terrible to her as the dark side of the moon: herself.

And that's done.

But not yet. I'm imagining in words, as they do out here. Odd, in a language that would fade from me in half a year if I didn't continually get it from outside. (And to you, who will know Polish and Yiddish only when I get back!) Maria-Dolores, innocent of either, is asleep in the next cabin, cranky at having to have so many times of the month in a month (and so irregularly too) "ridiculous even at fifteen, let alone twelve," she says to me in eloquent Spanish, in her dream. Bumble, snoring, was lively enough today to have instantly annexed Mrs. ———, not only out of self-defense but quite distinctly for revenge. I told Maria-Dolores and she said, "That doesn't make sense." I said when did Bumble ever make sense. So I will seal this up and mail it in a few days.

But how to end? (It's a custom here.) Why, in the style of Maria-Dolores's books. There are only three left, since she's taken to deliberately heaving the ones she's tired of out the porthole when I'm not around. And I really haven't the heart to quarrel with her; they *are* bad! Here's the first one, a little oddly written, *The Mystery of Nevada*, which is lying open under her bed:

Funny, them McCabes, don't look like a fambly even though there's suthin' you can't put a name to that sets 'em apart from other folks. An' they got hired hands from all over, Chinks an' niggers, (that's you, pulling the apron off me when someone comes, half-speaking, half-laughing, "Quick, gal!") *even Injuns. And why they stay up in them mountains all by their lonesome, God only knows.*

The second, very florid and lurid (it's called *The Mystery of Captain Satan*), has been kicked, closed, into a corner of the room (on the floor):

O reader, how can we contemplate this disordered

*soul without horror? Gifted with a knowledge of self and
others few mortals possess, he nevertheless ran the gamut
of vice! living like a parasite, cheating at cards, refusing to
aid the very race that bred him but instead inflicting elaborate mental tortures on an elderly gentleman who
strongly resembled his deceased papa, and using his kind's
incapability for parenthood* (I told Maria-Dolores this; she
merely shrugged, not in the least interested) *as an excuse
for indulging in unnatural—and what is worse, even
some natural!—lusts. What doom is stored up in Heaven
for these hard-hearted men and women, diabolically dis-
guised as men and women or vice-versa and therefore in-
visible to our eyes, speaking the language of anyone in the
room, which is dreadfully confusing because you can't tell
what degenerate nation (or race) they may come from,
and worst of all,* PRETENDING TO BE HUMAN BEINGS? WHEN IN
FACT THEY ARE??? (it goes on).

And here's the last, honorably placed on the table by
her bed. It's a remarkably quiet and gentle one (all things
considered) and she rather likes it. She's going to keep it.
It's called *The Mystery of the Young Gentleman* (he's a not-
so-young lady, we find out) and it ends accurately and simply, in a very old tradition:

They lived happily ever after.

"So *that's* it," said the schoolkid. "The world was saved by the telepathic minority, which gradually took over everything and once communication was telepathically perfect nobody hated anybody and there was no reason to fight any more."

"If you believe that," the tutor remarked, "you'd believe anything! No, it wasn't like that at all. In fact, the telepathic minority died out a few centuries later, without having influenced public events in the least. However, a Utopia was indeed established on earth only a few thousand years ago and now we're going to take a look at that Utopia."

"All right," said the schoolkid, "but no surprises this time or I'll turn you off."

And the schoolkid listened.

Bodies

Through these years it was not my mind that grew numb but my soul. An astonishing observation: it is precisely for feeling that one needs time and not for thought. . . . Feeling requires leisure. . . . A basic example: rolling 1½ kilos of small fish in flour, I am able to think, but as for feeling—no. . . . The smell is in the way, my sticky hands are in the way, the squirting oil is in the way, the fish are in the way. . . . Feeling is . . . more demanding than thought. . . . Feeling requires *strength.*

—ANNA TSETSAEYVA

Writing isn't talking. God damn it. Look, James, this isn't going to be an easy letter. I'm going to finish it, put it in the Net, turn my signal off, and go to bed. I'll be asleep by the time you get up, so don't call if you decide to answer your red light or just go looking for something intelligible to read or know about (little enough here for either of us). I keep thinking of the impulses in the Net as sparks flying underground or undersea or bouncing off satellites; of course it's faster than that. It's already morning in Hawaii and this will get to you almost instantaneously when I depress the Transmit key.

Which is a little daunting, the irreversibility.

Never mind.

Here the moon's setting over the desert as I write, round and pink as a giant peach. It'll be dawn soon. I've been out most of the night with the emergency work crew, doing the few unskilled jobs. South of us Pueblo has decided to celebrate some inexplicable historical holiday (they all know what it is but nobody here does) with an enormous bash and early tonight someone, probably lit up, ran a vehicle into one of our electrified fences and shorted out a whole section. Whereupon the lean, wild desert cattle came stampeding in, red of eye and mad of heart, like the power station mural someone did unknown years ago (and which we now have to face every time we eat in public), and trampled and tossed the solar collectors, goring some. We've been replacing them and fixing the fence. I came in for a good bit of random swearing—I'm not handy and have blisters—before Flowers got through by telephone to Pueblo (they were risking their happy bods with fireworks and not paying attention to any form of communication but the emergency lines, naturally) and chewed them out proper. Then everyone was ashamed about me (though it was pretty mild stuff like "Gosh!" and "Wow!" and "What bad work!"), but I turned sulky and held out for a new dining-room mural as the price of being pacified, and now Fill-up has typed out an order for one and we are to get a new muralist in a few weeks. (I don't think anyone can face the old one, anyway.)

Flowers and Fill-up came in a few minutes ago: "We're having a dress-up fit; can we borrow something?" "Not the orange," I said; "Anything else, but you clean it." They went off, beards wagging. And I thought: *I'll write James.* And I looked out of my window again, to see the full moon turning away from us (as it seems) and there was the dawn shift going to work. All those avenues and plazas left over from the old Heroic Age of architecture and the huge base of the power station—and eight little figures walking to and fro.

Hence this letter.

You don't remember but I saw you come out of the egg. I was there from the beginning; I used to visit you every winter when I was down that way. It never meant much past the first year or so—one can't anticipate something forever—but it was fun to see you go from a ball to a fish with a tail and so on—twenty years to make the full tour. It was odd to watch you re-living your first life under the transmission head; sometimes you were asleep, floating motionless as a lily in the tank like James of Shallot; sometimes they exercised you in your sleep; sometimes you were up in the air and in violent motion; you kicked and hit out, you ran, you talked vehemently, or sometimes just listened and looked. As a child you seemed often to be play-acting or posing. Later you cried a good deal.

All phantom.

I've told you: The memory must be fed in during real-time, just as the body has to develop in real motion; they can here, after a fashion, interpret the past-time EEG, but a moment's pattern takes weeks, even with computer analysis. Your connection with it was automatic; no one would really know you until you came out. No one knew me. They found us by looking for the one characteristic pattern and then grabbing us just before it happened; they can reach back for the DNA without using too much energy and the EEG takes even less because it's immaterial. Then they go forward, picking up a fully conscious pattern just before death, and trying to read it. They get some of it. Then they grow us and find out the rest.

The pattern is chronic misery.

Since you didn't ask, my first life was thirty-eight years in the Pacific Northwest: lots of greenery, close gray skies, low hills, cancer at thirty-nine. I speculated in—or rather, exploited others at—real estate and made a pile, rather unusually for a woman; you eventually wrote the story of your life. (Two such useless skills: moneymaking and autobiography!)

Since to them the difference between London in nineteen-thirty and Portland in nineteen-seventy hardly exists— we speak the same language, after all—they called me in. Your haircut. Your glasses. Why so little sexual activity? Why so many tears? "Let's greet him in the nude and pelt him with flowers as a gesture of friendship," they said, and I—upon whom that experiment had rather disastrously been tried—absolutely vetoed it for you.

You stood in the tank like a museum specimen in a showcase, your eyes wide open. You were the awkwardest human I've ever seen, graceless as an ostrich baby and quite as skinny, with your hair standing up as if you'd just been hatched and a piece of shell were still on your head. Then you made the big gasp, the *Ah!* to breathing air. I'd told them to break the connection during sleep (they got me at midday, driving downtown, because of some theory about peak physiological activity), so you woke from your London bedsitter—I would imagine—to find yourself standing in a transparent tank in what looked like a hospital room (my idea), facing white-gowned medical people, but of all the wrong races. I'd forgotten about that.

The immense discontinuity of that first shock. No, the—the *nothing* between.

You shook. The tank was draining; the water poured off you. You looked like Adam in terror. You looked suddenly rather lovely. Then you flapped your arms at us and wheezed something unintelligible; I thought, *Oh my God, they've scrambled him.* "What's your name?" I said, "Come on now!" and you backed off, trying to talk. Then you slipped on the tank floor, shouting, "I don't like this! I don't like this!" That—if you will remember—is when I opened the glass door, got down on the floor with you, and hauled you out, saying, "There's been a minor accident and you're in hospital. That's all. You're quite all right. Nothing's going to happen. Now who are you?"

You screamed "No!" and shook.

I thought my American was so rusty that you couldn't understand me. I thought you were crazy. I hadn't expected to like you, you know, and I suppose I didn't; what could you do at your best but remind me of a life I had no wish at all to remember? And I didn't then know your name and so couldn't connect it with your book: Jimmie Bunch whose Dad and Mumsie had threatened to put him away if he didn't quit the nail polish and the lipstick. Who thought it had happened at last.

So you huddled and cried. The lady who rushed back the curtains to show you the glass wall and the Rockies was King-of-Night, a machinist from Pekin. The banner ("Well-come, Time Travellor") had been flown from the Historical Institute at Paris. And the cat—Oh, Lord!—the first intelligible sound I'd heard when I arrived was not the strange human singsong "Ha-appakit! Ha-appakit!" but, clean as paint, the answering *Mraow* that explained it all: Happy Cat. Which I had told someone. So there she was.

You beamed. The cat landed on your bare feet and you shrieked. King-of-Night scooped her off and threw a *lei* round your neck; you giggled. The man I was talking to was George, the tall Asian from Chicago; he wanted to know: Why so afraid?

I could not—somehow—pour into that soft, vulnerably intent listening, that perpetual docility of theirs, answers like prison, commitment, beatings, electroshock, even lobotomy—or had they risen to that last in nineteen-thirty? Did anyone, James, long to go after your deviant frontal lobes with an ice pick? Well, it's absurdly embarrassing here when I tell some horror story and they don't condemn; I feel *on the wrong side.* And their knowledge is, in some areas, so unbreachably theoretical! I said you had broken our rules with your errant behavior.

What behavior? he wanted to know.

I said, "You won't notice it."

Names, exotic only to you and me. Just sound now. Like the light in Lucy, the uprising in *Oktobrina*. (But then you can't read phonetics, can you? although I finally did learn how to write them.)

Matching memories? O.K. The party, that night. James, scooting feverishly around the costume room in a trance of concentration, stopping every few minutes to look at his Awful Haircut in the glass. Whiz. Blunk. I never told you about the textile factory I once saw that was run by twelve-year-olds, did I? (They live alone, too, when they want.) You burrowed into the heap and came up with a gaudy green-and-pink kimono, your eyes shining, but Billie Joe in overalls, back from repair shift at the door said, Oh no, my dear. Blue and brown for pretty you.

You didn't understand, of course. You said, "Re-eally?" blinking. You have that trick of separating your words, a sort of holding action against possible unpleasantness, the perfect stopgap into which any sort of placatory meaning may insinuate itself. You widened your eyes and were good as gold. But Billie Joe, head tilted (kindly) to one side, held up pinkish palms covered with oil, said, flashing white teeth, Can't touch, and went away.

You didn't want to give it up. But I took advantage of your staring to twitch it from your fingers. I translated and you said doubtfully, "But men like loud colors," and then, "Will he be at the party?"

"She."

"Oh."

I said, "Everyone will, James. Put that down." But you

really wanted violent green chrysanthemums on pink sleaze. And henna-red hair. Or Art Deco and lipstick. I said, "James, nobody wears any of what you're thinking of, not any more.

"James, even the museums don't carry them.

"Look, James, if I don't stop you, you'll simply make a fool of yourself and not a man here will sleep with you. I *know* these people."

That caught you: a nineteen-year-old schoolboy hearing about Heaven. You looked as if something wonderful or terrible were going to happen, you didn't know which. You were turning painfully over and over in your fingers the edge of the blue blanket we'd put about you. Your (ill-fitting) glasses flashed. *May I? May I really?* You looked alabaster—not only the little RNA squiggles throughout you, my dear, but the mimicry of that climate you had (not really) lived in, and your fuzzy, light-brown masses of hair and surprisingly blue eyes, all very exotic on today's high New Mexico plains. And a moderately pretty face, I think, even though *non Angli sed angeli* is never going to apply to anyone, not in this world, not any more.

I think you saw permission in my face. Yours looked too stunned to be happy. Genetically, you know, you're not so much an opposite to Billie Joe's dark fullness and bean-shaped grown-up's eyes as a sort of side comment, an historically very peculiar (now) and quite irrelevant "What?" You were never allowed an adolescent's manners, I suspect, and I, at fifty, have been here too long to remember how to be properly middle-aged. But nobody cares for that any more. Not here.

I thought you were going to cry. Instead you said slowly:

"Make me beautiful."

The party.

I don't blame you. If six foot four of sunburnt blond

cowboy in range clothes came to carry me off, I'd go too. Especially with that handlebar mustache. ("I learn Henglish chust for you. I learn waltz-dance chust for you.") I thought: *Shall I tell James that this vision's name is Harriet? No.* So I was left with a list in my pocket of All the Other Things to Tell James, i.e.,

1. The hangings were borrowed, pearls and all.

2. We don't usually have parties in the central room of the old powerhouse—too big and the bas-reliefs are considered ugly.

3. The food didn't come in the usual way but was the work of an artist recruited from Denver, who took over our (usually idle) kitchen.

4. The three-inch flower-on-a-stalk rising out of the punch bowl (the one near the caviar) was our music-maker, an indirect descendant of the long-ago, dim gramophone. It uses the air itself as a resonating instrument, don't ask me how.

5. The funny-looking, bulgy-eyed cat with the soft pasted-down curls who was trying to play cat soccer by batting apple puffs into the soup was Billie Joe's pet, a hypoallergenic or Rex's Amber. (No guard hairs.) She jumped in the soup later, to the much giggling and gratification of the guests.

When you had died and gone to Heaven (I mean you two disappearing across the hall behind the arches—indeed, I actually saw your footsteps better than I saw you for nobody ever dusts the place and the desert wind can't be kept out of anything here) Madame Butterfly cried *He will come, I know it!* and I was claimed by the musician from Calcutta with whom I'll be reconstructing yet another opera. They like the music here and I tell them the stories don't matter. Then, when the party food was all gone, several of us descended into the bowels of the foodbank and unflashed some beef rolls; there was a lot of eating and drinking and a round dance between the freezers but no smooching—I suppose people weren't in the mood that night. Then the Marshmallow Giant appeared, shirttails shoved anyhow into his pants, wringing his hands and saying Young James Is Unhappy, Ogod. (I hadn't told him anything about you, you know; for one thing, I hadn't had the chance. And we don't confer.) Someone else I know came in between the row of tables, shouting enthusiastically, "I'm *exhausted!*" which proves that different temperaments still exist, which is reassuring, sometimes, and Harriet cried. "Move!" I said and he did—they always do—and I thumbed him away, didn't want him with me.

Where had it happened? Out in the desert under the moonlight, in a sleeping bag? Standing up behind an arch in the Grand Ballroom? Either you'd fled to your own room or been in it all along; what *I* saw was James Bunch sitting on his nice new bed platform in his nice new room, with half the potted plants tumbled out of their niches, the nice (new) orange sunburst quilt torn clean off the adobe wall, and the other bedclothes wound about him up to the ears. You glared. Your hair stood on end. Your nose and eyes were red. You looked like a caterpillar absolutely refusing to come out of the cocoon. I could smell the semen. Though why there were flowers (little orchids?) all over the floor and what looked like strips of pink silk chiffon hanging from the nice new furniture I really didn't know—unless all the pet cats in the powerhouse had come up to play Flower and Strips of Pink Chiffon Veiling Football for the last two hours—and clearly you'd been crying.

You shouted, "They're *Communists!*"

There followed eight-ten minutes' outraged diatribe, during which you gave a very good impersonation of someone else, probably your father.

Then you cried.

I said, "James, what's the matter?"

You cried some more.

I said—do you remember?—that I might not be able to understand but I would try and I thought you were lovely and Harriet was lovely, and after all, it was I who had introduced you.

You drew the blankets o'er thy young brow, as the song goes. Silence.

I said, "James, tell me."

You blew your nose convulsively under the blankets.

I said, "Look, my dear, did he scare you? Did he go too fast? Did he want you to do something you didn't want to do?"

You gave a dismissing sound, half cough, half snort.

.   I tried again. "He thinks you're very pretty."

You made an indignant sort of writhe.

"Well, if you don't want to tell me, I'll go," I said, which was mean, but it worked; you squeaked Yes and rocked a little. You seemed to feel better under the covers; yet it's odd receiving confidences from the top of someone's head. The head tossed a bit. First you had walked in the moonlight and H had kissed you and told you how beautiful you were (the romantic part), then you'd both gone up to your room and you'd finally allowed him to put his hands on you (this was the stammered part), and then you'd asked him to pretend that he was one of the Visigoth conquerors of Rome and you were a proud Roman patrician lad taken as a slave (that was the strips-of-veiling-tied-up part, I suppose), and then—

I ventured this, that, and the other about anal intercourse (knowing a few things about Harriet and having seen some of the sheets you'd been kicking about) and you shot up out of the bedclothes, breathless and tousled and glaring deep pink; I suspect you were hiding an erection. You said, fumbling among the sheets, "Where's my glasses?" and found them and put them on with shaking hands. Then you said, "He's not a *man.* It was horrible!"

(Ah, dear, if you'd only seen him riding the horses he trains!)

But you cried. You were outraged. You said he'd promised to do something special that you would really like and you must shut your eyes, and then he'd draped a sheet around himself and put on perfume, and stuck flowers all over the sheet and in his hair and on his bare skin (with tape). He had even tied two so that each dangled from an end of his handlebar mustache—the crowning horror.

Alas, you were not won over by the idea of a Flowering Harriet (I was, very) and tried—you little beast!—to kick him, which he hadn't told me, by the way— and you yelled and tore at his sheet (hence the flowers about the room) and then you threw yourself on the bed and screamed. Whereupon H came looking for me. James wants to be adored by a real man (thought I) and that will be hard on him in this world where the men and women all vanished years ago. It was very like tonight, you know; I mean a nearly full moon setting outside your window and some amateur star-gazer out with a telescope, trying to catch Venus in a hand-made twenty-inch mirror. I suppose it struck me—truly for the first time—that I was literally old enough to be your mother. I wanted to touch your hair but didn't dare, then. I tried to explain all this and you dove back under the covers, kicking your feet out in a temper of disappointment.

I said something like "Well, you see, there aren't any men and women, James, not any more. No one thinks that way any more."

I said, "James, it's all different now."

And then, after a moment, I said:

"It's been two thousand years."

But you switched the subject. You're good at that. Tossing the hair out of your eyes and dressing yourself in only your dignity and the blankets, you said:

"Oh, *that's* all right."

Then you said, consideringly:

"If they're Communists, then everything's free, isn't it?"

I said, "James, do you understand what I—" and you said promptly, "Of course I understand you." Then you added with conviction:

"I hate you. I never want to see you again. *Go away.*"

Not to be angry, not any more. Mind, if I'd known what you were up to, I'd have strangled you, my dear!—or locked you up and lied about it to everyone else—but I've always underestimated the Anglo-Saxon capacity for self-punishment. Imagine anyone else going out on the New Mexico desert before dawn without any clothes!—but you were in the company of a perfectly responsible and respectable (everyone is, here) musicologist from Calcutta who could even speak English, and you were at least clad in a quilt, not lost out on the desert and stiffening in the frost. And she would be (she was, of course) indulgent and forgiving and very concerned for your welfare because they're all like that here. And you didn't know—how could you?—that nothing needs such secretiveness here; there was no reason to sneak off like that.

Well it was a year ago.

Not so very angry.

Not any more.

Weeks and months Post James (P.J.) when nobody heard from you, but we certainly heard about you! Their talk isn't mean, you know, but they worried: Is James happy? Is he well? Is he enjoying himself? Do you think he's behaving that way sexually as a reaction to the too-little activity before? I would say, Yes, James mentioned to me how glad he was about that. Luckily, my James, your lower-middle-class upbringing limited your ideas about the sheer scale of mess one person can cause here. James and the Suds in the Swimming Pool, James and the Traveling Bonsai Collection (I admire your pertinacity, hauling pots from one shed to another all night, just ahead of the baffled judging committee!), James and the Red Spectacles on the Commemorative Sculptures of the African Whales, and so on.

There was a James Club. Nothing formal, you understand, but people kept dropping in and talking about you, a major way people keep track of one another here. I got romantic. I got proprietary. Imagine me talking to an earnest circle: James this and James that and I know, and no, he won't be coming back this winter, and yes, he has a temper, doesn't he? and yes, now he is Experimenting. It was the right distance, somehow, for that sort of thing. People showed up to chat while I was patching the dirigible slip (winters are icy with lots of thaws and re-freezings and just enough water to buckle a road surface) or learning to repair hovercraft, and when Flowers broke a shoulder falling off the balloon rig, we moved the whole business to the Pueblo hospital.

Then Ch'u Tz'u came to get me: James has come! And is not wearing a hat, he added in awe. We thought that you'd brought us presents, as people do: ornamental carp for the pool, cactus for the mall, a pocket music-player, wind-up calculators, things like that. And there you were.

You said, "I need such an enormous lot of things."

James, brown. James in shorts and hiking boots, James with silver sun-shields, with his shirt rolled up to the elbows. James, muscled. You were pulling with you, and had apparently learned the use of, a bicycle. Ch'u Tz'u wheeled excitedly away to tell everyone that James was living up to his reputation for interesting rudeness and you said, not even looking after the prosthetic, "Don't expect me to stay long." I suppose my expression must've resembled the musicologist's. When you left here without explanation I mean. Well, I know what lies behind the arrogance of young things and the exasperation at the claims it makes, which half the time leads to smacking the object in question. But you were (relatively speaking) decent enough on the walk back to the power station, like "Why do you stay here?" (wrinkling your nose at the place).

"Low stimulus level," I said. "I like deserts."

You said, "*I'm* keen on the cities." And then, "Still . . . all this sunlight!"

You added. "That's a good thing he's got, that wheeled thing."

I said, "Perhaps you like it better here now."

James grinned.

"I shall tell you all the places I've been," said this confident stranger. "I've been all over the world. Mumsie and Dads would be shocked to know the places I've been and the things I've done. Even back to Bayswater. It's a zoo place now; there are rhinoceri in the back garden."

"Eating the tea roses?" I said.

"Yes," said James promptly. Then you said, propping the bicycle against the powerhouse wall with a flourish, "They'll do anything for me here. They like me." With your pack half off the machine you remarked, "Would *you* do anything for me?" and then added politely, "I'd do anything for *you.*"

I said, "Don't leave the machine there"—*la mákkina,* slang for anything weighing under thirty-five pounds. You said, "Is there a cook here now?" which I took as an indirect way of saying, *Is it worth my while to stay to dinner?* Maybe you were only making conversation. But I remember too many conversations from my past that ran *What's for*

dinner? Let's fuck. Sorry, have to go now. You held out a fist
and opened it, saying, "This is for you"—it was that pho-
totropic paper kite which grew and grew in the sunlight, a
giant orange flower swaying up from your palm. I'd never
seen one before, you know. In the shadow of the doorway it
collapsed (most comically) back into a nut and I took it,
very pleased.

Then you said, "You'll have to pay for it," and do you
know, I almost gave it back! But you went on, "I mean by
showing me the mountains. Can we go on a holiday to Taos
and sleep out in a sleeping bag? I've never been."

I thought, *James is twenty.* (I say that to myself a lot.)
*He's only twenty and he doesn't know anything and it
doesn't mean anything.*

You said, your sun-shields flashing, your voice light,
"It'd be like the films. You know, *Rose Marie.*"

As we passed the indoor pool I said, "Don't throw
stones; there are fish in there."

You sang good-naturedly, *Rose Marie, I love you!*

Which was the newest, most glamorous thing, I suppose, last year when you were young.

Twenty centuries ago.

Billie Joe just came in and asked me what I was doing.
I said, The hard part.

Memories: the dead vulcanism of that part of the world,
the black cloud of the sagebrush stems over the ground. I
think you wanted to unsilver the top of the car, imagine—at
noon, in July, on the road to Taos! I don't actually remember much of our conversation on the way: What would happen if the Net ever went out (duplication, redundancy),
why the hotels were full (summer), various polite ways of
asking if we were there yet. I remembered another conversation, one I had had at the age of eight—"What's that?"

"Kansas." "*Still?*" Just before sunset the light went sulphurous yellow, turning very green the cow fields we could see through the trees to the south. And the mountains, ninety miles off.

You said, "It's very bare, isn't it?"

Then you said, "It was very hot, wasn't it?"

Then you started to smoke when it got chilly and we were in our blankets. And started to tell me, lying there and looking up at the trees, about the Tall Handsome Man. You were full of theories—he was "really" your father, you'd seen him repeatedly in the films, you'd come across him in the storybooks you and your girl cousins would act out when you were very young. All these together had ruined you. You talked as if you alone had invented the whole business. You said, "Find him for me."

Then you said, "Do you think you can? Will you try? For me?" but you didn't wait for an answer. You went on at length about the costumes you and your cousins had made out of bedspreads or other things—those little girls who are long dead, or rather they never really existed, did they, for you? I kept remembering how you had looked in the tank. It was all at one remove even then. In the middle of all this you slid your hand out from between your blankets and slipped it, with surprising gracefulness for one so young, under my shirt.

I said, "James, that's part of me. It's not padding."

"I know," you said. You were high enough to add, "I think *you* may be the Tall Handsome Man."

This is perhaps a good place to stop. I expect our opinions as to what came next will differ, especially after the lapse of a year. I didn't, contrary to what I'm sure you're sure, mind your staying quiet and letting me work; there's considerable pleasure in that for a woman who spent much of her growing up in a time and place that made that the one real taboo between women and men. But there was no pleasure at all in having James shut each eye in turn and focus the other experimentally at different distances, from right behind my head to (in stages) the tops of the eighty-foot-tall trees.

James, imitating a sofa pillow.

James, smirking.

Then you called me "little mother."

You also inquired politely whether I had finished yet.

Then, after I didn't finish but gave up, you remarked tearfully, leaning on one elbow, "I thought I'd *enjoy* that."

You came, my James, closer than you know to being abandoned right then and there, with nothing left you but your underwear. You could use it to wave at the helicopter that comes every day for the digs at Taos—archaeologists resurrecting the adobe Woolworth's where I remember buying tampons so many years ago.

Note: I did not leave you.

Second note: I did not wake you up in the middle of the night, as you later claimed. I let you sleep. In July the sun's up early and it's best to be moving early if one's going to walk. That's all.

Third: There's no town (any more). Those little houses for artists have been gone a mighty long time and both of us would have had to travel centuries to find them. I wasn't keeping them from you.

The dry wash and second growth likewise disappeared with the reforestation program long before my time; I wasn't hiding them.

Fourth note: The bus comes every two hours *from the sky*. I told you. If you wandered off instead of staying in the shelter, don't blame me.

And there was nothing for breakfast because James had raided the box the night before, after smoking, and had eaten everything.

James, describing his latest homosexual conquest in great detail and then asking me "what men like."

James, making wondering comments about the oddness of women's bodies.

James at the Bus Stop (looking interestedly about in every direction but the right one): "Are we going to take the bus?"

Myself: "No, James. You are."

Fifty is mortality time, believe me. If we were talking I could say it right, that as an (adopted) mother I've been something of a bust, that I'm (half) sorry, that I still don't want to give in or forgive. That I too spent my first year out of the tank getting it on with anyone who would, first the women (of course) and then the men.

Look, James, we may have it all now, but we'll never *have had it all.* That's why they can afford to be so soft. They part before us like the Red Sea! I used to think they had secrets, said things to each other that we weren't allowed to hear, had opinions of us they didn't show. They don't, of course.

But they do.

And I'm sorry. I'm truly sorry. (So I have said it at last.)

It's late. Billie Joe looked in earlier, saw me writing, smiled lovingly—don't they always—and went out again. I said to her, "Are you going to grow more people from the past in your tanks?" and she answered, *No. It's too sad.*

I made that up. It didn't happen.

Would you like a telegram saying, "Come home; all is forgiven"? I'll put one in the Net. Or be pleased to get one from you, you know. Children of our time "knew" that adulthood was like childhood, only better; twenty-year-olds (that's you) "knew" that at forty they'd have the same bodies, the same opinions, and the same emotions.

It wasn't true then.

It almost is now.

Come back, dear James. In time you'll know what I know at fifty but I haven't all that time, like you. People like us are so spectacular—all those sparks and edges—but it's only self-defense. It's the years of never getting what we needed, whether in the tank or in the past.

And it doesn't go away.

It's late. Your blond giant is out there on the desert, spinning slowly round and round with the skirt of his pink dress belling out and his hair and beard floating. He's dancing all by himself. The moon's setting. It's truly wonderful here almost twenty-four hours out of the twenty-four, I don't want in the least to deny or minimize that, but all the same, there aren't five people in North America who can speak our language.

Which wears, in time.

And for that twenty-fifth hour (which doesn't last long, by the way, only a few moments a day but it's there), *I don't really like them.*

There. I've said it.

Come back, James. I need your memories and your faults; you'll need mine someday. Come back and tell me how rotten it was—but who here knows or cares about that? In a few weeks I'll visit the Antarctic (another opera) and then back here for the winter. I was ill last autumn, briefly, with something that would've killed me in the old days; and I want as much of the desert now as I can get.

No, I am not ill (now).

No, I am not dying.

No, I will not be either (soon, in future).

It made me think, though.

Understand, James, this is no love affair. But you'll tell me about the time you were beaten up on the street, which is inconceivable here, and I'll contribute my horrors, and we can agree to be selfish, spectacular, demanding, sulky, defen-

sively unpleasant—and, in general, quite impossible—together.

The night shift is gone. The moon's in bed. Harry Yet
must have hypnotized himself. If I continue watching him,
he'll do it to me, too. There's not a sound out there, although the usual tremendous change (dawn) is going on—
with inconceivable speed and masses inconceivable, everything inconceivable.

Home, James.

I'll put this in the Net now. And take back what I said
earlier: *I hope it wakes you up.* I'll be awake if you want to
answer. Not much more to say; the spinning's getting to my
brain, I think, but I won't go on long, only end as we used to
on our letters—did you, too?—Some Place Some Time
Some Month Some Day Some Year Some Body, State: Of
Mind. Silly, eh? But here's the final significant word. I put no
"dear" at the beginning of this letter, but

I remain
at the end of it
without reservation
or qualification
most humbly
and sincerely
Yours.

The schoolkid had turned the tutor off and sat, brooding. Then after a while—snap!—and the tutor was on again.

"—to save the world," said the tutor, "or How Things Changed."

The schoolkid listened.

What Did You Do During the Revolution, Grandma?

We saw the lightning and that was the guns; and then we heard the thunder and that was the big guns; and then we heard the rain falling and that was the drops of blood falling; and when we came to get in the crops, it was dead men that we reaped.

—HARRIET TUBMAN

An army of lovers should be able to get out of bed.

—JILL JOHNSTON

Beloved Woman,

Before the apologists insist, as they are so fond of doing, that the tone of our ten years' correspondence is merely Victorian effusiveness—

No matter; the moon's up, dusty blood-orange over the desert, and the jackhammers are at last still. That massive piece of the New Prosperity they've been working at all day (it will be a solar power station, I'm told) begins to look almost bearable in the afterglow, though nothing but time and ruination will ever transform those grim heroics into

anything quaint or lovable. People are all over the patio
tonight with radios on their heads, and from one machine,
taken off for a moment, comes the news that our shot Head
of State is suffering from what the announcer calls, with
mystifying accuracy, a "spurious fever"—I report what I
hear, though no doubt the real phrase is entirely different. I
also convalesce comfortably in my deck chair, watching the
mountains, nose back to pug, fingernails growing out again,
hair an even dirtier blond (because of all the grey), and the
melanin fading, though at this altitude I'll inevitably keep
some of it. The new teeth hurt and I gum vitamin-filled por-
ridge. I even have "slaves" (the shifts rotate) to help my
hands heal. Fairy Marvin was out earlier today with a group
of tourists, bearing down on them as if he were herding
pigeons, smiling alarmingly with all his splendid muscles
bunched. You never met him so I will describe: F.M. is six
feet four, almost eggplant-colored, with long mauve fingernails and silver eye paint. He's not supposed to know anything or be capable of anything so officially he's a typist;
unofficially he uses his intimacy with the working of the
computer (a smile, all teeth and bulge: "Need someone? I'll
help out!") to dress in flowered gauze shirts, painfully tight
pants, and sequin-covered ties—all this by way of a personal
statement, which has gone unpunished in an out-of-the-way
place like this. One evening in the cafeteria (but it was before my time) he's supposed to have appeared with nothing
on but a tiny pair of pink gauze wings sprouting from between his shoulder blades, hence the nickname.

He's made us respectable. (He's running the tape of this
letter—dictated to a machine—through the computer for
me.) And considering the Social Security riots and the
shooting (did you know that employees were seizing busi-
nesses as early as *two centuries ago?*), I think there's no
harm in telling you what we've all been up to. Especially
now that F.M.'s private act of computer transformation—the

reason I'm still a respectable petty professional and not a jailbird—may turn out to be unnecessary.

To digress: Will you, O moon of my delight, send me a copy of *Las Tres Marias,* the forty-five-year-old edition? There's only microfiche here, which irritates the quick of my fingers, and narrow-band illumination, which turns my eyes to boiled onions, much to the awe of my students (I've been given an exercise class to keep me quiet), who ascribe the latter phenomenon to the care and concern with which I watch them make fools of themselves; "Yes I can!" they shout at trek time and then collapse with hypoxia.

To stop digressing: Your excellent brain has ignored the science of shifting and *Ru* potential only because you've always had better things to do—my knowledge of politics, for example, has always made you wince—so I'll be brief.

Imagine a hypersphere.

You can't? Well, neither can I (as I say to the tourists when I give my little tour in the Dome), but it's mathematically provable that we live on one, i.e., on the surface of the four-dimensional regular solid described by the motion of a three-dimensional (or ordinary) sphere moving through an additional (fourth!) dimension. I'll mostly skip the backup, which demonstrates only that a point moving in one dimension creates a line; a line moving in two, a plane, a plane moving in three, a regular solid; and so on. The name for a four-dimensional cube is a tesseract, or rather the thing's image projected in three dimensions, as one may draw a three-dimensional figure (say, a cube) on the (two-dimensional) surface of a sheet of paper. And on this hypersphere, we—I mean our entire universe, you, me, Fairy Marvin, the gatepost, and the farthest stars—are located at the one position where the relation of cause to effect is absolute and absolutely reliable: 1.0 *Ru.*

What lies on the rest of the surface of the hypersphere? For one thing, the universe from which we draw our raw materials and power—*Ru* ± 0.873 or lower. Those worlds beyond *Ru* ± 0.742 are inaccessible—instruments sent there freeze, burn, or explode quite at random— while for those between ± 0.999 (and so on) and about ± 0.931 (all of these, of course, run to a finite but very large number of decimal places, many more than I can indicate here) the differences between them and us are too small to make exploration practical, since the last thing we want is to meet Mrs. Bedonebyasyoudid coming back round the corner. Between ± 0.921 ± 0.877 or so we're dealing with people who, although more or less like ourselves, are nonetheless very unthreatening, technologically speaking, and from ± 0.877 out, we find unpeopled Earths, paradises of exploitability.

All very lovely (you say) but where's the catch?

Here: *Ru* is a *consistency* measurement. Only at *Ru* 1.0 is there an ironclad relation of cause and effect. It's this that permits travel "outward"; *we* travel but the ± 0.999 worlds don't. Below 1.0 the meshing of effect and cause grows loose and sleazy, while reality itself grows more and more thin. It's as if the universes were not so well machined in some places as in others. Tourists, by the way, *like* the idea that we live at *Ru* 1.0; it pleases them to think that our Earth is the only one in the entire hyperspherical cosmos to be totally consistent, totally determined, and (as it were) totally real.

It doesn't please me.

Did you ever hear the old joke about the optimist and the pessimist who both believed that this was the best of all possible worlds?

There's a religious group somewhere in Chicago which declares that Hell is located around the circumference (equator?) of the hypercosmos, a perfect ± 0.00000 and that we, at 1.0, are in Heaven—an idea to give one the cold staggers, I think.

That's most of what I understand of the whole eerie business. To add: Moving objects "inward" (towards 1.0) consumes energy; moving them "outward" (away from 1.0) liberates it—our energy-hungry new industries are based on the throwing "outward" of hydrogen atoms, our raw materials on the expending of almost—but not quite—as much energy bringing metals, timber, and what-have-you "inwards." So none of this is (as much of) a free lunch as it's represented in the media. I'm told that changes in *Ru* are observable only at the subatomic level until one gets out farther than is physically safe; but I think the anthropologists and sociologists could tell a different story—cumulative inaccuracies showing up first in human symbolic structures, those most intangible of patternings: language, culture, tradition. Farther out, towards the Rim, things are too unstable for even these to survive and there rather abruptly ceases to be anything recognizable as people; still farther out life itself vanishes. All this suggests to me the irresistible speculation that we, like Plato's cave shadows, are merely the ghosts of ghosts. Imagine being *read*, so to speak, by someone from *Ru* 1.0 as if you were only a character in a bad play—and did you know that extras in crowd scenes in the movies don't actually talk? They count or repeat nonsense syllables, just as unreal as can be. Which is something like existing at a low *Ru*, I would think—though we, at 1.0, are safe.

About my other theory you may judge for yourself.

This is how it happened: I was called for during my elementary self-defense class. Why it's assumed the emigrants will need self-defense deponent knoweth not, but they get it every morning with their cereal and their egg substitute; and I, with my rejuvenated fifty-eight-year-old body, creakily teach it. One of the authorities was an unfashionable fellow with a bright red tie, outsized shoes, and a booming voice—so, you see, I'm only a little fish after all. Or perhaps he was their scientist.

He said, *We want you to do this little thing for us: go into Storybook Land and impersonate an ambassador to King Shahriyar*—but this really means a two-bit less-than-medieval Earth which I studied briefly some years ago as part of an anthropological-cum-linguistic backup team. The ambassador (they said) was ill. He's not; he's dead. I know that now. And I can never see in these official types anything but the projection of anonymous and expensive power; they aren't individual enough to be people. So I replied very carefully, *O great king live forever, thy servant's use of the tongue of that place was long ago.*

He said, "We'll give you time to brush up."

O ruler of rulers (said I) *before whom all lands abase and destroy themselves, for how long will this condition of things persist?*

"Seven days," said he.

Oh god (said I as I had said before) *who controllest the sun and the moon, will not the Ruritanese, being a patriarchal bunch, despise thine humble servant?*

He said, *We'll fix that.*

And they did fix it, truly, making my face as black as night; and for my fingers fashioned they talons of fine silver; filèd silver fashioned they for my teeth, and mine eyes too were silver and my hair was likewise tangled lank and long of the same color—

There is, in Ruritanese mythology (my own nickname, you know, from Ruritania) an arch-demon of the pantheon, *Issa,* who is very like our own Asmodeus, Lord of the Flies, whose Hebrew name is Ashmedai. A picture of the arch-fiend (he's a rapist among his other endearing qualities) can be found in a picture-book I helped put together years ago after that other expedition (my name's not on it). I sat with that book in my lap, surrounded by technicians—technicians are as nice as the real authorities are nasty—leafing through for an alias. What matters about disguise is the fantasy in the head, the opportunity to go crazy in your own way. I had been through the book five times and stopped at Ashmedai four; I said, "That one."

Shock. Surprise. Doubt.

I said, "Look, with my height I can't possibly pass, but it's right for him. And you don't want something similar to the Ruris; you want something entirely different. That way they won't notice details. And not black—swarthy—the 'Tani are more blond than me, more brave than you—we don't want to strain their credulity too far. With this get-up they won't care if I'm a man or a baboon; they'll be too busy snatching the kids away. And they'll *remember*." So will I. I have never had such an unpleasant and complicated time in my life. Cosmetics had viruses bred for the silver, easy enough on nails and hair but potentially dangerous elsewhere and it settles not on the (blue, as I hope you remember) iris but on the round, white eyeball, turning it silver—a very eerie, empty look. The skin is also a simple, not-quite-harmless parasite, which had to be hooked to a specialized *penicillium* with *E. coli* and the result settled in my digestive tract to avoid flare-ups. The new teeth hurt. The claws were another graft and then, while the cosmeticians rested, we had our long consultation with the weapons people. But I'll keep that for a surprise. I said to F.M., while waiting for the nails to stiffen, the hair to grow (some of it merely dyed), my eyes to settle down and stop being weepy and red (I was putting desensitizer on my new teeth for they, too, pained me), "All this for a week!"

"Why not?" said Marvin. He was making himself useful, as usual, sorting through a box of Ashmedaian belongings. "Here," he said, handing me a painted miniature of a demon princess, accommodated as far as possible to Ruri notions of beauty and the fantasy that the men of any alien race are always hideous but the women infinitely desirable—have you noticed?

And neither of us ever mentioned the worst absurdities: my age (dear God!) and, oh yes, that my nose had been reconstructed to a super-Semitic beak, symbolic of what I absolutely refused to let them add below, or the rank upon rank of scarlet Ruri war medals, for they do have them, only as jewels, not ribbons.

Marvin rummaged on in the heap of Ashmedai belongings, still holding the miniature out to me.

He said, "Wear it next your heart."

Issa is amazingly ugly. Imagine the Ruritanese male costume as Kabuki and you won't go far wrong; first there's the long, boxy *ob,* over this the elaborately folded and stiffened *lena,* and around both the layer upon layer of the padded and heavily embroidered *vistula.* In really cold weather— for Ru $+0.892437521$ is always cold—a thick sleeveless overgarment called the *bug* is added. But I'm playing tricks; you will recognize, I hope, the names of Russian rivers? Ashmedai wears black, or black and silver, or black and scarlet, very Byronic. And I actually learned how to fold myself into all that junk, underneath which you can't tell if it's a man or a giraffe, so prudish are the 'Tani, far worse than your ancestors and mine. After my teeth and nose and fingers had healed, after I'd re-mastered the language tapes, after the electronic systems in the jewelry had been tested and retested, after I'd been checked for the tenth time for infection, and for the tenth time cleared, after I'd gotten dressed and undressed without a mirror a dozen times, after the weapons people had opened the skin under my ear and closed it again, after my palms had healed, after I had memorized a sketchy account of the geography, history, religion, customs, architecture, and weather of the Kingdom of Faery (from which place I was supposed to come) and the last black sequin had been sewn on the last black *vistula*, the last piece of jet prised from its setting and placed over printed circuits—

A Kabuki actor looks in a full-length mirror for the first time, just before going onstage, to see the objective image, the *persona* of his role. Marvin (who gets in everywhere) said, "Darling, it's *you*," and catalyzed the room's nervousness; the technicians snickered.

I looked.

What can I say? In the mirror was a monster, a Prince of Darkness, some great Lord of Hell, swarthy, talon'd, cruel and empty-eyed. Rubies flowed and flamed on his breast. What I can't convey, my dear, are my emotions upon seeing this creature; as Goethe says, to put the inside outside and the outside inside! I thought, *They'll know. They'll see,* and the indecency of it made my knees buckle. Marvin said, "You're a Faery prince," and I, in a voice that modulated from a harsh, penetrating whisper to a high, choked scream: *Silence! Issa speaks!* I saw the image strongly flex and then relax those fearful ringed talons. Seven short days!

Need I tell you that Ashmedai is beautiful?

A first look at the Ruritanese peninsula: rainy, dark, and cold. Tall firs under a sky the color of milk and potato soup. The underbrush is a mess of rhododendron and fern. I step down from the shift platform to the drenched grass of a clearing somewhere near the sea; yards away behind blowing fog are the shapes of my 'Tani servants, warned of my arrival by the sudden shower of light that is an artifact of the shift system, in this fog only a masked and unlocatable glow. There's a strong smell of wet wool. I step forward, the black *ob* hampering my movements, thinking crazily that it's only a movie on location, that they're not real, that somewhere (just out of sight behind the trees) Eisenstein is filming us. My first visual impression of them reinforces my belief; they stand in a line like a still out of *Alexander Nevsky,* and then one comes forward and flings himself down on the wet heather. The others follow, old sacks, brown and grey, topped by broad white faces from which the November fog has taken all color. I say, *Rise,* a guttural followed by a throat-twisting click, and the horse they're leading—I used to ride, years ago, and hated it—shies at the sight of the ill-smelling, worse-looking stranger and has to be blinkered and held while I clumsily mount. The wind shifts, bringing the smell of the sea. There's a weight pressing down—dark and impalpable—which, it takes me some moments to realize, is the sky. I said—forgive me, but I did; in Ruri this is the ordinary salutation of courtesy and one hears it many times in the course of a single day—

Take me to your leader.

What shall I call the 'Tanese I know? Their names are full of buzzes and clicks. Some words are easy: *evar,* the archer; *gorad,* castle; *driv,* a huntsman. You can imagine the rest (so why talk about it?), the dark fir forest, the outer walls, the archway we passed under, the bare stone corridors lit by torches, the Great Hall's huge fire and long tables, the crude splendor of the courtiers, the ladies of Ruritania even more elaborately and richly dressed than the gentlemen, "like beds of flowers," says an old chronicler. It's a gaudy heap of red and blue. Then there's the plain food during dinner, the endless songs (all quarter-tones and innumerable verses) while the men vie with each other to make indecent remarks and the ladies throw dried fruit. All this through a haze of adrenalin. After dinner the Princess Charlene sang, King Fred's only child, a motherless thirteen-year-old with the round-backed matronly body and velvety brown eyes of a baby Judy Garland, and the same power of projecting enough emotion to knock you over; certain young nobles (Count Al, Duke Joe) remarked loudly, "That

Princess Charlene is one swell little artist," and "That Princess Charlene sure can sing, all right, all right." If it were summer (this is Al's nervously fashionable neighbor, the Countess Debbi, on my left, in not quite as many different colors as the Princess but more than any other woman in the room) they'd have held Play Day in my honor: drinking and wrestling in the woods, ball games, teenage nobles chasing between the trees swans too young to fly. Count Al said, "Why is a raven like a writing desk?"—I approximate the Ruritanese—and Count Sid, "Because both are anonymous constructs!" (or something like that) and everyone roared except the ladies, who tittered.

It went on and on.

And on.

Seven days of this.

Snapshots: four frightened men holding a black mare for Ashmedai to mount, the panicky beast edging back towards the courtyard wall, Issa's talons slipping badly on the black leather reins. Confidential rides by the sea and preprogrammed conversation with the lean, old, professionally eager Court Wizard, my contact this-side. A stocky, dull apprentice putting a sleep spell on my bed, my asking, "How does that work?" (*Imitative or sympathetic? Come on, fella, you have to have some theory; no answer and it's three more semesters of Elementary Magic for you*) and, after long reflection, his baffled reply: "Nobody knows." An interlude in the Court chapel before a perfectly awful gilt picture of The Game God and The Fish Provider, everyone praying and looking very hard at me. Ashmedai's nails and dentition striking terror to the hearts of gardener and busboy as I've never been able to do in the classroom. An unexpectedly clear sunset at four o'clock, reddening the ivy that climbs the walls of the kitchen garden, and an aristocratic 'Tanese toddler bursting from the marigolds to make straight for me, legs pumping hard—only to be snatched from the path at the eleventh instant by a young lady in a brown, servant's smock, almost a baby herself—waitress? factory hand? typist?—who braved horror and certain death to rescue somebody else's child.

They're real, these people we abuse and exploit.

I lie nightly in the private tent of my leather bed-curtains; Issa is praying to his strange gods. Figures of animals and spirits, painted on the leather, dance crazily in the light from the tallow dip. From the rubies on my wrist, tiny and clear comes the voice of Fairy Marvin, my contact that-side:

". . . what the Maoist said to the Stalinist . . .

". . . looks like at last . . .

". . . we of the Lavender Left understand. . . .

". . . stay a full year. Instructions from the United Front."

I whisper, untruthfully, "Marvin, I can't hear you!" Communing with spirits. I can feel the weight of the castle over me, stone on stone. No baths, bad food, secrecy, everything I care about a world away. Outside would be the rainy state of Washington if there were such an entity, but here there are only peasants and forests, mile upon mile. Moreover this is the only kingdom in the only inhabited continent in the entire world—to the south the 'Tanese nobles hunt tribesmen who live behind wooden palisades; to the north and east are the mountains; and beyond that there is nobody at all, an empty continent, the sheer craziness of $Ru + 0.8$.

Marvin says hurriedly, "He's dead. He's been assassinated. That's why they wanted you. Now you're to stay but you'll take your instructions from us. It's very important."

He adds, "Good luck, dear!"

And Issa—betrayed by his familiar and cast out from the Kingdom of Faery—

—weeps.

How I met the Princess Charlene:

I noticed her the first night, singing her heart out.

She wasn't as good as Victoria de los Angeles but she was the best (certainly) that the place had to offer.

Her father, King Fred, asked me to teach her mathematics (arithmetic).

This made the Court Wizard sulk—maths was *his* job.

Her Duenna—

But you can imagine it already: that woman's age, her stockiness, her suspicions, her missing front tooth, the piece of rose-colored embroidery on which she's always working, the little Princess making eyes at me across the inlaid table in my private apartments; hangings, stone, the floating-wick lamp.

I thought of teaching her set theory but couldn't remember it, possibly the effect of *Ru* + 0.8 on the brain. Though she was a good little scholar.

"I can't *do* nine times nine!"

So I taught her to add and multiply by casting out tens.

She said, "Tell me about Faeryland."

I said, "The castles are slenderer and more beautiful than here; the brooks run wine." ("*Nothing* is more beautiful than here," she says firmly.) "We ride gryphons. I'm engaged to a High Queen of Faery; here's her portrait" (taking out the miniature). "Her name is Aloys."

"Is she more beautiful than me?" says the Princess.

I say, accurately ambiguous, "Your Majesty silences me."

By the fifth lesson (hunting for my knee under the table): "But surely Your Majesty finds me ugly?" She says,

pouting like mad, "You're *different.* Civilized." Tokens
brought by little servant boys in brown smocks (the language of flowers and leaves), pale abstracted looks, sighing,
the traces of tears. By the seventh lesson she claims to have
forgotten the multiplication table ("I'll never use those silly
numbers anyway; what I need is to learn about *life"*) and at
the eighth there is a dramatic scene where the Duenna—
pale and resolute—slaps the Princess. The two women then
exchanged a glance of complicity, looking fearfully and
guiltily at me (their judge), both crying out at once.

The Duenna: "She made me do it!"

The Princess: "She's lying! She's jealous because she's
old! She's thirty!"

What to do but see them apart?

The Duenna says (with a profound curtsey), "Sir, I'm
the daughter of a poor goldsmith. I'm not a noble. I'm thirty;
nobody will look at me any more. If you report me, my life's
over."

The Princess says, crying and clinging to me, "Do you
love me? Do you love me?"

I think, *Thirteen is sixteen here.*

She says helplessly, tears on her lashes, "You've mag-
icked me!"

Twenty, really.

"Kiss me!" she cries; "Oh, kiss me before she comes
back!" and then excitedly, after I do, "Will you take me to
Faery? Will you? Will you marry me?"

I'm old enough to be her—no, her *great* grandmother.

And they burn folks for practicing magic, here.

How I became acquainted with the Lords Art and Bob:
A tavern built into the outside wall of the castle and lit
by smoky torches, hidden by trees. A relief from the tedium
of the long winter nights. Seventeen-year-old Bob and nine-

teen-year-old Art, both very blond, both drinking, are both in love with the thin, nervous Countess Debbi, Bob purely but Art *par amours.*

Art says, "Look! There's the great Prince Ashmedai."

Bob: "I want to assert myself, Art."

Art: "Better not, Bob."

I've been here before, been through all this before. The tables are carved with initials like sophomores' desks; the horseplay's the same (chug-a-lugging beer in the corner). I've seen the faces in a dozen fraternities, at twenty mixers and hops.

Bob says, "You have a—an *accent!*"

The foreign prince is astonishingly ugly but has magnificent jewels and implacable poise. *Tace, daemon.* But it wouldn't.

Bob: "The Countess Debbi is the most beautiful and desirable woman in the world!"

I said politely (bowing) that the lovely Countess Debbi (who habitually threw bread crumbs down my back by way of seduction) was worthy any man's praise.

Bob said, "No, sir, the most beautiful. Of any!"

Art said, under his breath, "Watch it, Bob!"

Bob said, encouraged by his buddy's presence, "If you don't like her you're a ———. You haven't got a ———. Fight, you bastard!"

Issa never fights. Issa can do better. Ashmedai, from one heavily-jeweled forefinger (black diamonds, jet, blood rubies), loosed a bolt of tame Faery lightning that crackled to the astonished forehead of the Lord Bob. Between the effects of surprise, pain, and fear that noble Lord fell from his wooden stool to the stone floor, disgracing himself.

I said, *I can do more.*

Drinking with Bob and Art, I told them of Aloys, High Queen of Faery, so jealous of me that she'd rendered my

Queen of Faery, so jealous of me that she'd rendered my male member unworkable with any lady save herself. That she was the mistress of unimaginable sexual skills. Of excruciating pleasures infinitely prolonged (I got that from a movie ad). That those who fucked as they did with a peasant girl, until your belt buckle burst, were missing the best part. That Queen Aloys could kill a man with her merciless expertise. That she could spend an entire night caressing a man from his head to his feet with lips, body, and tongue, during which time he would suffer the little death not once but many times, over and over. That her breasts were heavy, her back round, her waist small, her navel deep, her neck long, her nipples pointed, her lips scarlet, and her vagina wriggling and voluptuous. That for one night of her love a man would gladly undergo a year's abstinence. That he (Art) and he (Bob) had not the stamina to survive her.

Lord Art shouted eagerly that the 'Tanese would invade Faery, conquer it, and possess all the women.

Ashmedai grinned.

Lord Bob declared that he wouldn't have such a thing known about himself for anything.

Ah, but I have magic, too, I say, and then Issa tells of the horrible toothed vagina that devours lovers. The unsatisfied Queen no man in Faery dare approach. Pacing her chamber with more than human passion, her inflamed vulva throbbing, her violet eyes dark with torment, her hands on the curtain of the bed where she's doomed to lie alone because of you-know-what.

Art cries, banging his tankard on the table, "I'd fill her hole for her!" and the Lord Bob, troubled, denies that his fidelity to the Countess Debbi has in any way been shaken.

Later the younger generation, aspiring to this lady or that, approach me for advice. The (useful) rumor that

Aloys's glamour has been laid upon my privates so that to anyone in Ruritania they'd look as if they weren't there——
——like a woman's.

Bob says, "I love the Countess Debbi with a pure love, but how can you be certain your love is pure, you know? And how can you tell for sure what women feel about you or what they want?"

The Lords Art and Bob, pining with love, decide to get a peasant girl. So we slog for half a day through the eastern forests where blades rust and spiders spin their webs, dim vistas of decay pacing us as we ride. At a thatch-roofed hut on the edge of fields we dismount and they confer anxiously, kidding and boasting. Then Art kicks open the door and, foolish and flushed, Art and Bob jostle each other; this is the hut (they say) of Crazy Sherry, who does it for free, that unfortunate member of the working classes who hid behind the door when she saw us coming and who's now lying on the floor and trembling. One table, one bench, one firepit, some straw bedding, a heap of rush matting, half finished for market; this is her elegant furniture.

"This woman is mine!" whispers Issa hoarsely. "Out, both!" and I draw the sword I don't—really—know how to use.

Bob, not so dumb, protests.

Art does the same.

I say:

She's doomed. Can't you see it? She's had her courses for thirty days and will for thirty days more—women's magic put on her by a neighbor over some base peasant matter, the theft of a pig or cow. I need this curse to drown Queen Aloys's spell and thus take my pleasure, but you it would slay. Do you want this one's sick, evil flesh to touch your most intimate part?

Art puts one hand over his mouth, nauseated.

Bob isn't so sure.

Try then, I say, stepping forward and locking eyes with him, good mammalian politics even at $Ru + 0.8$ and I add, "Dost like to fuck in blood?" for of this, Ruri men are not only queasy but genuinely terrified, believing that it causes every catastrophe from impotence to dandruff to plague.

Issa adds, *As for me, I like it. But I don't like to be watched,* and I lift my sword.

Bob hesitates.

Art grabs his arm.

They go out, finally.

Finita la commedia—I mean they'll watch, of course, out or in, so how will Issa Do It? On top of Crazy Sherry, miming intercourse and trying to explain the situation in all but full view on the dirt floor of that neat, bare, excruciatingly primitive little dwelling. She's too frightened to hear. Leaving her, lacing myself, I remark to empty air that any man who touches her within a period of thirty days risks a lingering disease that will cause his member to drop off.

Art has hysterics (outside).

Bob explains, giggling: "Her *husband!*"

Then there's an argument on the way back: *Was* that Crazy Sherry or not? Bob says no. Art says yes. Bob says somebody laid a spell on us and we found the wrong hut; Art then says it was the right hut but the wrong woman. Later in the declining afternoon there's another wrangle— shall we follow another forest path to a second hut?—but Art, seriously annoyed, refuses. In the west, over the trees, is a flaming magenta sunset of the kind the Princess Charlene has already declared to be (in front of the whole Court) "spiritually beautiful." Bob maintains earnestly that the forest holds all kinds of creatures—giants, water spirits, demons, men whose heads grow beneath their shoulders—and tells stories about them the rest of the way back, each one ending, "And then he slipped it to her."

And I, thinking of all my other failures, with the weight of the sky on my head, whistle all the way home.

Where are the children? Where you would expect them least, in service, at trades, at hunts or feasts. They're independent at seven, adult at thirteen, old at thirty. Only old King Fred and the Court Wizard, at forty, fit our idea of adults. Noble babies, hidden in country houses and private apartments, were loosed on us for the Solstice Festival, which is seventeen days of prayers to the Holy Fishing Rod (its catch, the Sun), the Play God, and Baby Lady, avatar of the (usual) matriarchal-religion-before-this-one. There were skits and games. Lots of drinking. I invented checkers and was voted Most Popular. Princess Charlene (tipsy) kirtled up her skirts to play hopscotch and the Court gossiped for a week. I' the mazes of the dance—but it wasn't graceful, as you imagine; it's clumping, bumping, country sort of stuff— she says archly to me, "Did you know, a rush-mat maker was killed by her husband because she was pregnant by one of our men and then the husband killed himself?"—but thank God it's Countess Debbi of the plucked eyebrows and ex-ophthalmic eagerness who gives me this seductive tidbit. Then we change partners and it's the Princess who says, "What's the matter?" Clump. Bump. Walk up. Walk back.

She adds affably (the way people always do with this particular bit of news), "You look terrible."

Hop. Hop. Hop.

She says matter-of-factly, "Have you drunk too much? Do you want to vomit?" Jump. Turnaround. Walk up. Walk back. Fairy Marvin is far, far away.

"Tell me," she says.

She isn't shocked—rules of behavior don't apply to relations with the lower classes—but she wonders at my bothering about somebody else's deeds.

Now is a good time to stop.

Instead I tell her.

Hop hop hop.

She says, "To spare—?" and then suddenly, kindling and glowing, "To spare his lady the pain of even that disloyalty"—walk up, walk back—"and yet remain polite to his friends!"

Jump.

I mention the peasant—

"Oh, *her*," says the Princess. "Yes, of course, but his *lady*—"

Change partners.

Over the nuts and candied fruit, a discussion of the Faery women with a whole bevy of ladies, their fashions, their dogs (gryphons and gryphonettes), their pastimes and games (remarkably like the Ruris'). Their age? "I'm fifty-eight, Madame" (truthfully), and I show all the subtle signs of age and none of the obvious ones, which only increases my beardless strangeness in Ruri eyes. And then:

Drat!

The Brat!

She's been bribing her Duenna to keep watch while we smooch, so here comes the part you've no doubt been waiting for—the Princess, clad only in her glittering low bodice, her heavily tucked skirt, her three frilled underskirts, her two plain overskirts with their floating panels of embroidered thick silk (traded from the southern barbarians), her stout corset, her silk chemise, her lacy *grundoon* (or bosom-kerchief) of thinnest lawn, all these in different and very clashing colors, and no underpants, in my bed at night. Thank goodness the Ruri have no personal parasites, a happenstance for which I've often been extremely grateful.

She whispers, "I am Yours."

"Take me," she breathes.

Then, "*Can* you take me?" she says, and I, "Alas, lady"— and she—and I—and she—and I—and then a very awkward silence.

Then I say, "There's a way—"

Very incautious of Issa, no doubt, but how can you throw a lady out of bed? Especially one so highly connected? And under all those skirts beats—but her heart's not under her skirts and the whole topic's indecent; I didn't come here to masturbate a thirteen-year-old.

On the other hand—

She's really rather sweet, asking me in a trembling voice if I'll pretend to be a pirate, brutally ravishing her, so I throw all those skirts half over her face (to avoid quite suffocating her and yet give her the weight of fabric she insists on, quite the oddest sexual requirement I've ever met) and grasp her little moss-rose and take her halfway to pleasure— how quaint! *pirates*—! as if she had a secret yen for polka-dotted socks or cuckoo clocks or panties embroidered with the days of the week in red thread.

Trembling harder, she begs me to stop.

"Then take off those silly clothes," I say, brutally in character—

—thinking, *Maybe a knee?*—

—no, I doubt she'd buy it.

And she sheds the Princess, red all over and face averted, and having found nakedness even more deliciously shameful than pirates, lies there while I violate her with my mouth, which (thank God) makes talking impossible.

She jerks, crying out, "What went wrong! What went wrong!"

I laugh, hairs between my teeth, can't help it. She says, wondering, "Is *that it?* It's not so much." Then she adds, "But it is."

I put my fingers inside her; she groans and then, moving

her hips from side to side, "Oh no. Oh, don't. Oh, please don't."

So it begins all over again.

Count Sid also begins to hang around, to fool around with the stranger. They throw a basketball together after hours. His hero-worship. His sullenness. His drinking. His insistence on my company. His loving nobody *par amours.* Friends until some fancied slight enraged him, some instability in his own character, unable to stand the demon-prince's tall delicacy, his slenderness, his dark foreignness. Were there dreams from which he waked shuddering? Suspicions: Was the Faery playing some horrible double game? Planning some terrible betrayal?

And then the news.

Count Sid, very pale, stands very straight (with a tic in one eye) in a rough stone hallway of the castle, under the guttering torches. Outside, fog fills the scented spring night, rhododendron and camellia blooming under the trees as in a terrarium. He says passionately, "You traitor!"

And Issa, all silk and subtlety:

Thou, who lovest me?

He says, "I know you're up to something, damn you for a sneaky traitor, damn you, damn you, damn you!"

Thou sayest falsely, by my soul.

He says, "I know this at least, you're sleeping with the Princess, aren't you, you stinking bastard! You stinking, murdering, faithless bastard, everyone knows it!"

He says, more quietly then, "I'm going to tell the King."

So nervous, so jumpy, so tense, in such mortal conflict is Count Sid that a single blow will down him. Sid's easy. Issa measures self against that fair, muscular obstinacy, his sweating, bearded face, his broad shoulders, his Ruritanian good looks. Issa smiles.

I challenge thee.

The King, who doesn't like my scheme for colonizing the eastern interior (orders from headquarters): *Don't.*

The Court Wizard, who just doesn't like me, period: *Don't.*

So I did.

The Ruri love it; it's a mirror image of what happens in the bedroom, I suppose, where someone must be *unseated* or *unhorsed* or *pierced.* Then there are the banners and the massed chivalry and the colorfulness in the stands, but you can imagine all that. I'm fingering behind my left ear, just in case, my that-side gift (God bless the technicians) now sunk into bone. Forever mine now. Here's my conference with Fairy Marvin the night before:

Marvin, you know I can't tangle with these youngsters physically.

Marvin, I want it.

Get me the arming code.

Do you want your very special agent—

I'll undress in front of the King!

That's better.

I've chosen no weapons at all and no horse, astounding everybody, and now as I go up to shake hands with my opponent—the grass, the trees, the mild spring sunshine (we won't see the sun again for months, most likely) just as in the movies—there, on the Challenger's Stool, on the Challenger's Blanket, innocent of double motives or cloudy conscience—you can see it in his cheerful, good-natured face—sits Lord Bob. Beaming. Thus it is to have middle-aged eyes. He says apologetically, "Sid's sick," and the stands roar.

He outweighs me by a hundred pounds.

I say—but I don't, having planned to drop into Count Sid's morbid, utterly sensitive ear some ultimate homosexual obscenity, to make him (at the very least) mad and careless. I go back to my place, inadvertently stepping on some of the camellias the Ruritanese ladies have begun to throw onto the field; milliners' waxy-looking flowers, totally artificial in their pink and white and striped red, somehow the climax of all this absurd pageantry. Training with the device surgically implanted in my skull was an eerie process of self-hypnosis, first on pentothal, then, for reasons I don't profess to understand, on acetylsalicylic acid, finally on nothing.

How it happens: At first the color values reverse themselves; then for a moment they disappear; when they return everything's accurate but too bright, as in migraine.

Then there's the high singing in one's ears—climbing blood pressure, a danger to middle-aged arteries—and an indescribably awful headache clawing up one side of my skull.

Then I stop seeing—nothing as simple as things going black, but a progressive white-out in which details twin themselves and blur and then my whole visual field loses its depth. After that the visual field's still there but I can't, somehow, attend to it—and then some sixth sense, very tactile, suddenly becomes obtrusive, and I direct my pain to that rift in the senseless visual picture that means life, at first with great difficulty but then as part of an uncontrollable pain-relieving process, quite out of my power to stop or slow down, all of it taking place down in my gut and simultaneously right up against my eyes.

I've killed mice like that, disrupted their brains and opened lesions all over their bodies—I don't know how.

And then it's over.

There's a stretch of grass before me, some flowers fallen on it varying from white to pink to red, and the edge of the stands, all quite ordinary. There's the comparatively weak pain of migraine, and my left eye almost obscured by pale-blue blotches while across the whole lovely day are the characteristic scintillating stars of *scotoma.*

The heap of flowers, with some difficulty, some internal dissension, resolves itself into a fallen man.

It's very quiet.

I say something—possibly that I'm not to blame for her supernatural pregnancy—to the dead rush-mat maker, who's suddenly there for a moment, doing something on her way somewhere.

I don't remember whether or not she said anything back.

I don't remember feeling anything much except the pain.

I do remember the extraordinary quiet—that of a crowd *not* moving or making noise, you know?—quite different from the absence of a crowd or the presence of a few folks—and then the slow, low, heart-destroying roar as the crowd, at last, woke up.

And I remember the face of the Court Wizard, secretly pleased as he came towards me. I am, it seems—his staff is stretched out in front of him for protection—lying down. Hated by the nobles now, hated by the peasants, and quite out of magic.

And I never felt less like Ashmedai in my life.

He came back.

After the quarantine in the forester's hut—

After the attack of the demon soldiery of Faery's hereditary enemy, the Kingdom of Graustark (F.M. and the typing pool), through the mist and the camellia-laden undergrowth—

After the battle for possession of the Princess (staged outside Her Majesty's royal apartments), each of us shouting instructions to the other in English—

After the moment in the arched stone corridor, before the door hung with Her Majesty's colors, when Ashmedai, Prince of Faery, spread his arms wide to ward off or absorb

into his own person the harsh and unintelligible curses of
the black Graustarkian demon—

—and was skewered through both open palms.

Glamorously, heroically, horribly convincing, utterly re-
habilitated, pinned by two needle-like daggers to the Princess's door. The one part the 'Tanese surgeons can safely be
allowed to treat. Local anesthetic or I couldn't write this
now.

He hung there, fainting.

Then there were tears on his face, dropped from the
eyes of the little Princess as she knelt by the side of her
fallen champion. Refusing (thus did the demon) all aid but
the Court Wizard's, who tended him during the next few
hours, through the shock and the fever, through the pain,
through the night of no sleep, through the double vision
when I covered one eye and tried to read a mash note from
the Princess Charlene but was defeated by her spelling—

—and couldn't bear to move my hands and so cried
and swore at my own wretchedness and the impossibility of
contacting F.M.—

—who came through anyway. Issa was lying shivering
and wrapped in blankets on the floor of the Great Hall. Terrified that the Princess Charlene would *take my hand,*
which she did, and so I fell into that dark, slippery, icy-cold
cave of fever that I had been dreading all along.

Then it was F.M.'s face bending over me: kindly, compe-
tent, concerned. Tiled walls, fluorescent light, white garments like Heaven. Voices I'd known years before in an
earlier life.

Demerol and silence.

The next day brought us all the extraordinary news: *We
are not at Ru 1.0.*

Mind you, it's not that any form of relativism has replaced the hierarchical conception of order formerly insisted upon; there's a center at *Ru* 1.0., all right.

But we're not in it.

Imagine: *to be read* (as it were) by some other, some superior mind from that Heavenly place where effect and cause dovetail absolutely!

Who can—unlike you and me—look up at the night sky or think of our Sun's Phoenix reaction with something approaching confidence.

Even Marvin's kindness can't—even my adventures among the 'Tanese can't—make up for that.

It's also clear now that the stability of the entire super-cosmic hypersphere is being badly endangered by our cheap power and inexhaustible resources; only the inhabitants of *Ru* 1.0 can play such games and get away with it—and they, it seems, don't want to.

So we're not so different from the Ruritanese, not any more.

O Beloved, *what is it like* at *Ru* 1.0? I can think of nothing else. The euphoria of a successful revolution (with which I had little to do, as it turns out; my urging King Fred to colonize the eastern interior is now absolutely useless to anybody except the Ruritanese upper classes, who will be free from now on to do exactly as they please) ought to banish such thoughts, but they will sneak in.

Imagine: Reality's like mountain-climbing, except that as you reach the precise altitude of the absolute illumination, as you move out of the deceitful blurring of the atmosphere, you also cease to breathe.

Or like coming out of the water when you've been swimming, a dropping-away of that friendly support, the sounds around you suddenly harsh, the chilliness, the gooseflesh, the drag of increased weight, all this in a desperately thin medium which doesn't prevent you falling and skinning your knees, or (even) smashing something.

Let go. That's wisdom (they say). I'll stick where I am, let my hands heal, and hide from tourists. Maybe I don't want to get out of the water anyway. After all, at *Ru* 1.0, where every effect follows perfectly from every perfect cause, our little Cause might've got lost in the shuffle; I might've missed the Princess Charlene, poor old Sid, Bob and Al the Disgusting Twins, high-strung Debbi with her pop eyes, or poor Crazy Sherry. I think: *Crazy Sherry might be alive.*

But then I think also that I might not—O never discount this as mere Victorian effusiveness, You Who Come After; human pleasures, human pains and human loves are real, not rhetorical, no matter on what *Ru* position of what more-or-less Earth they occur; they are the only things that count and would reconcile me to a great deal more than any small nuisance I have to put up with in this newly-emerged, post-revolutionary, stumbling, bumbling, not so very dreadful, indeed rather nice and quite significant Utopia-to-be—

I might not have—

you.

"—little things, ordinary acts—
"—Rome wasn't built in a—
"—banal—"
The schoolkid said, "I don't believe you."
And listened.

Everyday Depressions

It's *all* science fiction.

—CAROL EMSHWILLER

Sex Through Paint

—WALL GRAFFITO (PAINTED)

Dear Susanillamilla,

Lady Sappho in curly gold letters is the name of the book I will (will not) write.

Gaywyck turned up in the Gothic section of the bookstore this morning as I was looking for Marvin Harris's (Poly Sci) *Cultural Materialism*—title in lavender (*Gaywyck*, not Harris), mysterious mansion in the background with one window lit, in the foreground (near the sea) a dark & dashing Byronic gentleman in riding boots looking down at the place where the heroine ought to be, but instead we have a delicate and lovely Blond Youth. Mine will have two Ladies.

May I thrash the plot out with you?

At the "a" in "illamilla" my dark heroine developed a name; she is Lady Mary de Soyecourt who writes poems in Greek (hence the nickname of the title). Her father is Lord de Soyecourt (will you please ask you-know-who if this is possible), Norman blood, mutant (sort of) aristocrat, admired Mary Wollstonecraft and educated his daughter as if she'd been a boy. He was also a "natural philosopher" (i.e., scientist, chemist actually), was a friend of Lavoisier and got mixed up in (the proper side of, i.e., against the aristocracy but not an "extremist"—i.e., not exactly for the peasantry either) the French Revolution. I must look up some of this. Flower beds and conservatories and Chippendale plates (?) and ancient oaks and estates and roomettes and so on. Lady M's mama was a Sheldon of Deepdene, Alice Tiptree by name, brought from the mild climate of Devon to die of a consumption bred by the rigors of a Yorkshire winter in the huge unheated de Soyecourt castle on the moors. (Ask Eleanor is the castle possible.) Only before she died (Alice) she bore two children, fraternal twins Richard and Mary, Richard the elder by ten minutes. Both parents are dead now and the children (Richard is heavily into debt—gambles—takes laudanum—drinks—has inherited his mother's weak chest—coughs a lot) have grown up under the guardianship of their wicked uncle William de Soyecourt, the younger brother of M & R's dead father, who controls Richard (nominally head of the estate) thru R's gambling debts, ill-health, and so on.

The estate is—by now—very poor.

Old de Soyecourt died ten years ago, in a riding accident, when Mary was fifteen.

Mary does not believe it was an accident.

Having, though, little evidence on which to base her suspicion of foul play, Mary remains silent on the subject. She spends her time doing chemical experiments with mercuric oxide in her father's laboratory, which is full of blown glass vessels and slate-topped counters (must check this) and whatever predated the Bunsen burner. Mary is trying to determine the nature of phlogiston. (Must try to find all this in the library.)

Uncle William, who is going to be either bullying and

lecherous or prissy and nervous (which do you like?)—but
if prissy and nervous he has to be Alice Tiptree's elder
brother, who was given the living of the place. That is, he's a
clergyman. The Tiptrees are gentry but not aristocracy, you
see. And if p & n (prissy & nervous) he'll be much in the
company of a Lord Doricourt from London, the real villain,
who's dissolute and raffish & whom Uncle William loathes
because he's being blackmailed by him (Uncle Wm. by Lord
D). Lord D is very useful because he can also rape a village
seamstress or try to rape her or insult—not Lady M, you
know, the other heroine, the blond one.

   I need a Heroine name.

Dear Susannawall (supportive, no?),
   Here it is. Hold on to your hat.
   Into this tangle of blackmail, secrecy, and danger (back
cover blurb) comes:
   Miss FANNY GOODWOOD from a shabby-genteel (but
affect'nate) family in East Wessex.
   Lady Mary had hired her (Fanny) to catalogue all the
books in the library (I have stolen this from *Gaywyck*, so
will have to think up something else)—no, run the village
school started by Lady M, who has radical—even Chart-
ist!?—leanings. (All that are compatible with running an estate, that is.)
   Now I need an estate name. Pemberley? Woking?
Bother?
   Bother was always loveliest in the spring. . . .
   Alice Tiptree (by the way) died of a broken heart. It
was one of those eighteenth-century Romantic Friendships
between women, marked on both sides by passionate
fidelity, a lot of reading books together, and volumes of correspondence. Ambitious Mr. & Mrs. Tiptree forced their
daughter to marry de Soyecourt, who (poor fellow) little
guessed the source of his bride's settled despondency &

tried unceasingly (but without the slightest success) to assuage her sorrow. She dies of consumption on a sofa, but first she has the twins—born in a forest in the Italian Alps—mother rushed out in a fit of hysterical misery during a storm—gave birth in a pine forest, in a peasant hut, attended only by an old gypsy woman. Now the SECRET (aha!!!) is that Richard was not the *elder* of the twins but the YOUNGER by some minutes, which only Uncle William knows because he got there just in time—everybody else was out beating the bushes to find poor lady S —— (Lady A ——?). Anyway he bribes the peasant woman (and has to keep on doing so) to say it was Richard who was born first, BECAUSE Mary and Richard's rotten old grandfather (who was a sexist pig & whose wife left him after three months because of his cruelty and coarseness), left the estate to Mary's dad *only under the proviso* that the firstborn be a boy. All this gives William much potential power over his brother (or brother-in-law) and even more over Richard & Mary. It is *even* possible (if you like; do you?) that Uncle W has had old de Soyecourt killed when blackmailing him didn't succeed, i.e., Wm. tried to blackmail de S and de S sent for the police (or whatever is the eighteenth-century equivalent) and William hired ruffians to do his brother (or brother-in-law) in. And *that* is Lord D's hold over him (William); he knows (or maybe did the job himself).

A genuine, first-class, 24-carat Gothic SECRET! P.S. Is there an East Wessex? (West Sussex?) Must find out.

Dear Susicle:

I have got enough plot to start now. As of last night Miss Fanny Goodwood was in an uncomfortably crowded public coach, and was, with each revolution of the wheels, coming closer and closer to the Italian correspondence hidden among the books in the library. By sheer chance (on the third day of her visit) Fanny will find the Italian correspondence in a copy of *Corinne* and will innocently mention it at dinner. And although ignorant of Latin and Greek, Fanny *is very fluent in the modern languages.* That's when the attempts on her life begin.

Do you think "he"—guess who!—can hold up the coach?

Too much too soon? Maybe.

Nonetheless it is Lady Mary (who grew up wild and tomboyish on the moors) who stops the coach, masked & with pistols cocked, demanding that the passengers "stand and deliver"—but no, she will take nothing from them but a kiss from the pretty lady in the corner (Fanny). This really ought to be, once I get the details invented, a perfectly smashing scene. Imagine our slight, fair, pretty (but brave) heroine confronting our wild, dark, Byronic other hero(ine), made angry by the demand, and yet Fanny feels a strange, intuitive sympathy for this dashing lad (for so Mary seems to her), the lace on whose wrists sends an inexplicable thrill through Fanny's sober brown poplin sleeve as "Jamie Campbell" leans in through the coach window. Perhaps it is Fanny, emboldened by she knows not what, who seizes the boy's head and imprints a kiss on the strangely smooth cheek—perhaps it's Mary who blushes. At any rate, Fanny is oddly disappointed when "he" gallops off across the moors.

But then at Pemberley Lady M is a strange and shambling figure, stooped and hoarse-voiced, wearing a linen duster, a mobcap, and green spectacles, the very image of an eccentric old maid. Fanny writes in her diary:

Lady Mary is so odd! But then she is so very good-humour'd and kind, so very Cultivated and so very well read that I find myself Curiously inclined to her. Poor Lady! She has little company save mine and that of her brother and Uncle, the last seems Tedious and Unpleasant enough, not what, I imagine, she cou'd wish. . . .

There follow long talks together, a visit to Alice Tiptree's portrait in the family gallery, where we see Lady Mary weep behind her green spectacles. Then there is Fanny's rapture at having a bedroom all to herself (*I fancy myself an Empress on her Throne! though to be sure 'tis a great empty room, and but slightly furnished, that is, in such Condition as sorts with the rest of the Castle—*) mixed with homesickness for her poor but jolly family (all of this she puts in her diary) plus tours of the estate with Lady M, who does the actual day-by-day work of supervision while Richard enjoys the exotic dreams of the opium-addict (lying on his bed), reads in the damp garden (coughing), or feverishly attends the wild gambling parties held by Uncle William in a small mansion he (Wm.) has rented on the edge of Town. (Yes, brutal and lecherous!) Slowly the two women become friends, but Fanny's growing happiness cannot blind her to Mary's strange exhibition of the contrary emotion, the times of unaccountable sombreness (or even real misery) which come over Mary in response to the most innocent act or speech. F writes in her diary, *At last I have a Freind!* [sic] *and one truly worthy of the Name! How can one so Learn'd and Good and of such High Position find it in her heart to love a person so Plain and Undistinguished as myself? It is impossible. Yet she does!!!!!*

Once, attempting to be cheerful but failing rather badly, Lady Mary takes Miss Goodwood to the village to visit two seamstresses there who are Mary's friends, one hard and angular, one short and turnip-shaped, both in their thirties (i.e., middle-aged), who have lived together for ten years and who know Mary better than she knows herself, i.e., they spot her and Fanny instantly, and discuss with them how much the Treasures of True Friendship surpass the Gilded Perils and Illusory Joys of that mistaken Passion miscall'd Love, whose unpleasing pangs are so often the agent of Woman's Ruin, and of Distresses too painful to mention.

Then, after M & F have left their (the seamstresses') frugally appointed (but tasteful) lodgings, Angle teases Turnip (or vice versa) about the flightiness and promiscuity so common among Female Friendships in London. (Ring in Mrs. Manley's exposés here and 18th-century women's clubs.)

To bed, and dream up the next plot wrinkle.

P.S. Did you know that some Elizabethan ladies scandalized the gentlemen of that age by dressing as men—except for the codpiece, which they wore about their necks? Truth!

Dear Suz:

A BALL!!! (I am glad to report.) Fanny can now take up pages and pages, worrying about her clothes (lots of description of clothes here) and Uncle William (brutal & hardy) will make her miserable (his intention) by mocking his niece, i.e., describing how Lady M will be there in spectacles and duster.

But—as if you didn't know!—Lady Mary here sheds her drab disguise and is not only revealed (to Fanny) as the creatrix of "Jamie Campbell," but is almost shockingly Handsome in cherry-colour'd satin and her mother's jewels (emeralds). Her face is radiant, her Form well-proportioned and elastick, her smile bewitching, her eyes sparkling, and her gait and manner everything that is most graceful.

Both ladies refuse the attentions of handsome young gentlemen (need names!) of the neighborhood in order to sit & talk together.

They exchange Memories of Childhood and reveal to each other the inmost Secrets of their Hearts.

The intimacy between them is remarked upon by the whole Neighborhood.

They are constantly interrupted in this delightful Employm't by gentlemen who wish to stand up with them, so before the Ball is quite over, Lady Mary says she has a dread-

ful headache and the two ladies repair to the deserted but-
tery (pantry?), Lady Mary revealing that "she cou'd not,
during the progress of the Ball, stand up with that very one
whom her heart favour'd above all others"—Fanny is over-
come but represses her tears—Mary reveals that she means
Fanny—Fanny weeps—then they waltz around the pantry
amongst the pickled meats and jam jars, exchanging Vows of
Eternal Freindship.

Then something happens.

Slowly the atmosphere changes.

They feel awkward and yet elated.

They draw closer together.

There are tears in Lady Mary's eyes.

Fanny is also on the verge of tears, but doesn't know
why.

Diamonds (passed on for generations from mother to
daughter) gleam (like frozen tears) on Lady Mary's neck.

Both tremble.

It is their first kiss.

Fanny (in her white dress and gold locket with its miniature of *her* mother) is innocently delighted; she takes the
kiss and her new feelings as the natural consequence and
accompaniment of lifelong friendship.

But Lady Mary, smiting her brow in agony, tears herself
from Fanny's embrace and rushes off despairingly, leaving
Fanny grieved and puzzled.

For Mary, like her Uncle, has a Guilty Secret.

But what is it?

My Old,

Bless you! Of course! Mary's secret is SEX!!!

Years before, at the age of twenty-one, Mary had another friend, a Miss Bethel, who shunned her (Mary) upon
discovering that their feelings for each other were carnal.
Taken on a holiday to the Alps by parents who disapproved

of Lady M's influence over their daughter (they wouldn't have minded if she'd been rich; they were trying to marry off Miss B to a wealthy brewer), poor Sophia, miserable, detesting the brewer and loathing herself, solved all her problems at one go by leaping off an Alp. Lady M, having been the innocent instigator of the carnal behavior, of course feels responsible for Miss B's death. Sex, you see, is not only unspeakably evil in itself; it leads inevitably to SUICIDE.

Thus tormented, Mary tries to avoid Fanny in the days that follow & poor F is hurt and puzzled, and after a while Mary herself can't stand it. So life runs on at Woking, with scenes of the village school (Fanny is, naturally, a born teacher and loves her little charges. Does she have any class consciousness? No), a disquisition on the good & bad effects of opium, Mary appealing to Richard *not* to go on smoking it in his rooms, Richard gambling (totally dependent on Uncle William financially and emotionally), the ladies out on the moors, talking about Women's Rights (which shocks Fanny at first but then wins her enthusiastic assent, quote Wollstonecraft), M vaguely Shelleyan about a future Utopia in which no one will be poor or ill, but sudden silences if Fanny mentions the Alps—or friendship—or Mary's past— or being twenty-one—tortured moments in which "the guilty look" (as Fanny calls it to herself) comes over Mary's face and she says desperately cynical things about life, to Fanny's consternation. I must also invent William's constant censure of Mary (a *much* bigger field for this if he's prissy and nervous), and the more and more frequent attempts on Fanny's life—breathlessly exploring the unused rooms and passageways of the castle with nothing but a candle, which suddenly goes out; F on the crumbling edge of a moorland cliff, almost pushed over by a figure she can only glimpse out of the corner of her eye; F luckily waking in the middle of the night to find that the hangings of her bed have been set on fire, and so on. Mary intercedes repeatedly with cruel

Uncle William on behalf of the local farmers and working people, etc. In an attempt to find out who almost killed Fanny on several occasions, Mary takes her newest (but dearest) friend to the moorland cottage of Old Ellen, Alice Tiptree's faithful old nurse. Old Ellen (or "auld Ellen" as I will call her in the finished ms.) is very old and wise, the local wisewoman who practices *wicca* and heals the peasants. Her cottage has a thatched roof and a lovely little garden all set about with stock and wallflowers. Or possibly it's all rude & wild, only a small plot of medicinal herbs marking the spot as a human habitation, and a habitation (to boot) of one conversant with the Old Religion.

Thus on & on. I haven't, Old Bone, yet come to the explanation (and may never). But the dramatic CLIMAX of the story is a DUEL between "Jamie Campbell" and the decadent and vicious Lord Doricourt, from London. Or, if necessary, brutal Uncle William himself. Mary has finally found out Uncle William's Terrible Secret! The two rage through the library, smashing ornamental vases, toppling antique bookcases, and accidentally treading upon and tearing priceless first editions. In the heat of the fight, in response to her antagonist's sneers, "he" throws off "his" disguise and reveals "his" true identity to the astonished villain. Uncle William (or Lord Doricourt if need be) then reveals to Mary what he (or they?) consider the unspeakable wickedness of the history of Alice Tiptree. This revelation unnerves Lady Mary (but not the reader, who has known it all along) who thereupon loses her weapon & sustains a slashed hand (or shoulder) and it is FANNY who courageously dispatches the villain.

She pots him with a candlestick. Or a vase.

He yet breathes.

I have long thought—she writes in her journal—*that false modesty is the only effective Obstacle to the emancipation of my Sex. The world labels Indelicate any action poor Woman may perform that displays Decision and Strength of Mind. Modesty I therefore believe to be a Syren's Song, to which we must wisely turn a deaf'n'd Ear. The truth is that in any Turmoil or Strife, be it large or small, Delicate or not, an English Lady is equal to anything.*

Dear Old Bone,
     Yes, indeed!
     Mary has vanished, stung to horrible guilt and despair by William's revelation—not only is she (M) accursed in herself; her stain is an inherited one and therefore inevitable. Fanny, luckily, is wise enough to seek her friend at the cottage of Old Ellen where—can you doubt it?—Mary has sought refuge.
     At this point we are going to have a *perfectly lovely scene* with wise Old Ellen (all that *wicca* and herbs, you know), who catechizes them both about their love for each other. (This is the positive-feedback-loop trick where not only does each get to recapitulate all the high points of the story, but they also get to react to each other's stories, thus providing the reader with even more reasons to get sentimental and weepy.) Then Ellen, to whom Mary has never dared to speak about this side of her life, reveals that there's an illegitimate strain of Highland blood in the Tiptrees, which is why she has been so devoted to Alice, who is really her second niece twice removed. Then she tells them that sex between women is O.K. (Ancient *Wicca* Knowledge). Lady Mary quotes the last line of Dante's *Paradiso.* Fanny says, "Oh you old silly; was *that* all? We used to do it all the time at school!" Old Ellen then has a speech, like this:
     Aye, lass, tak' thy sweet-heart, tak' thy jo. Gae nae waly ane tae ither . . . et cetera (stolen from Robert Burns).
     So!
     Love triumphs.
     And then? Uncle William repents, a broken man. Hardly

himself, humbled & timid (either because of the revelation
of his dishonesty or the crack on the head—Mary inclines to
the latter opinion, Fanny to the former), he soon retires,
either to a private sanitorium (if they had any then) or a
small living on the coast, where he labors unceasingly to be
useful and to repent of his sins. Richard, after a few months
of living with his sister and Fanny in Devon (where they go
because of the mild climate and Richard's weak lungs) and
showing a moderate talent for water-color painting, dies.

His last days are peaceful and happy.

The estate, now proved to be very rich indeed, goes to
a distant relation, leaving Mary nothing but a small legacy
from her mother. Then my two heroines, like the Ladies of
Llangollen, retire to a small cottage in Wales where they
spend the rest of their happy and uneventful lives. I may put
in a love scene here—though it's awfully late in the story—
no, should be earlier—but the pronouns get so confusing.

And then?

A walk into the sunset, hand in hand, and the obligatory
prophecy that Some Day Society Will Accept a Love Like
Ours. . . .

I know, I know, Uncle William has a split personality
and I should be researching the lives of Turnip & Angle, not
wallowing in this romantic garbage. Instead of nattering on
about her entirely revolting devotion to the aristocracy, Old
Ellen should be unionizing the dairymaids and inspiring the
local working people to throw their wooden shoes into the
new power looms just installed in the local textile mill. Lady
Mary is a cliché and an idiot, and Fanny Goodwood *is* wood,
and what on earth do I think I'm doing with a fair heroine
and a dark heroine—creating a pair of matching book-ends?
And there's nothing in it about racism, which is certainly a
more pressing concern right now than cherry-colour'd satin
& dancing in the pantry.

You are right; the book should be full of real politics,

but Oh Susannah, what wishest thou? Marxism-Leninism?
Too doctrinaire. Women's Studies? Too respectable. Lesbian
separatism? Too unrealistic. The "women's community"?
Too incestuous. Anti-racism? Too narrow. Cultural anarch-
ism? Too crazy. Gay liberation? Too many realtors. Doing
nothing? Too bourgeois. Marxist-Leninist academic lesbian
feminist socialist culturally anarchistic separatist anti-racist
revolutionaries? Too few.

Other lists I enjoy: croissants, pain au chocolat,
brioches (with or without raisins), madeleines, even whole-
wheat bread ("pain complet") in our new, local, wonderful
French bakery.

Cha-Shu-Bow (transcendental steamed buns with bar-
becued pork inside) ditto, a new Chinese deli, likewise.

I tell myself about these whenever I decide to emigrate
to Mars.

You have been a grand help, and I have a new raincoat,
lilac-colored and beautiful (but beautifully expensive, too)
which helps console one in Seattle as the days draw in, the
fog gets colder, and cars switch their headlights on at three
P.M. But six months from now it will be light at ten P.M.—
and I won't be able to sleep before three in the morning.

When I was twenty I thought that life came to a point
in some openly dramatic way (like in the movies) and somehow you got into adulthood at some point and then you
were set, on a plateau that went on forever and ever. Remember the contralto in *Pirates of Penzance,* accused of
being old and of having wrinkles and gray hair? And she
defends herself by saying (singing, rather), "They gradually
got so." When I was twenty-five and sang in the chorus, my
mother laughed and laughed at that line and I wondered
why.

Now I look in the mirror and see my mother.

What's it all about, Sooz? I don't know.

Middle-aged tolerance is hardly the thing to come to after such very technicolored expectations as you and I had!

But the shop stocks nothing else nowadays.

Oh yes! My love to Dennis. If *I* were a lesbian separatist with an ailing car, I'd bring it to him to fix. (How many lesbian separatist friends with ailing cars do you have now?) And love to dreamy young Nathan.

Last week a frosh wombun (wumyn? wymeen?) came up to me while the other twenty-year-olds were chasing Frisbees on the University grass, playing & sporting with their brand-new adult bodies, and said, "O Teachur, what will save the world?" and I said, "I don't know."

But that is too grim.

So here are some profound and transcendental truths about Life.

What is Life?

Is it anything?

Who invented it and when?

Is it patented? (If so, what#?)

Why does it always turn green in the wash?

When does the guarantee run out?

Does Life exist?

Well, yes. It does. Life is, well life is . . . like this & like that & like that & like this & like nothing & like everything.

That's what life is.

Live, if you have the time.

Etc.

Etc.

Etc.

Etc.

Etc.

Etc.

With Love

P.S. Nah, I won't write the silly book.

P.P.S. and on

"All right," said the schoolkid. "This is the last time and you'd better tell the truth.

"*Is that the way the world was saved?*"

The tutor said, "What makes you think the world's ever been saved?"

But that's too grim.

&c.